Holly

"Club Leader"

The Secret Three

The Secret Three

By Eleanore Hubbard Wilson

WITH

ILLUSTRATIONS BY THE AUTHOR

LOTHROP, LEE & SHEPARD CO., INC.
NEW YORK, N. Y.

TO MY SON
Eric

CONTENTS

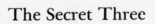

The Secret Three

The Calendar

Eric Lee was waiting for his Dad to come home for dinner. His blond head was pressed against the window and he stared hard through the dark. He wanted to catch the first glimpse of his father when he turned off the street into the walk leading to the apartment house where the Lees lived.

The apartment house was very big and built around three sides of a square. The Lees lived in the center, so when Eric looked out of his living room window he could see on either side the lighted windows of other people's apart-

1

ments shining like stars in the black night. Because it was just a few weeks after Christmas the apartment house reminded him of a big Christmas tree trimmed with many strings of bulbs. Wouldn't it be something to have a Christmas tree so tall and wide that it almost filled the sky!

At last Eric's father appeared, walking with his springy step, and yes, his pocket was bulging! Eric ran to the door before the doorbell rang. His mother came, too, wiping her hands on her apron.

"Hi, Dad!" Eric reached for the papers to look for the funnies and Dad leaned over to kiss Mother. "Did you bring me a present?" Eric was grinning because he could see it himself, sticking out of Dad's pocket.

"Just a minute, just a minute, let a fellow get his coat off!" His father ducked in the hall closet, then tossed the cylinder-shaped parcel to his son.

"Not exactly a present," he said, "but these came in the mail today and I thought you and Tony might like them." Tony Felipe lived in the apartment across the hall and he was one of Eric's best friends.

Eric tore the paper away from the long tube-like package while his mother watched over his shoulder.

"Calendars!" she exclaimed, "My, what fancy ones!"

"Gee Dad, thanks!" Eric looked admiringly at the picture on the cover which showed January. There was a snowy scene on the top of the page above the thirty-one squares for the days, and a cloud of silver snowflakes all around the edge.

"Where shall I hang it, Mums?"

"Why in your own room, I should think," his mother suggested and went back with him to find a place. Eric was proud of his room. It had wood paneling instead of wall paper, and a painting that his Dad had made hung on the wall. There were shelves under the windows for his books and guns. His bow and arrows and ack-ack rifle stood in one corner and his lasso was on the closet door. There was one chest of drawers for clothes and one for things like trains, erector set, or anything he wanted to put in it. His table was pretty well scarred with cuts from his carving tools but stood sturdily before the windows. His studio bed and radio were in one corner. It was a good room to do things in and it was all his own.

"I think here at the bottom of your pin-up board would be a good place for the calendar," Mrs. Lee said, and she fastened it there with thumb tacks. She stood back to consider the effect.

"You know, there is something wonderful about a calendar, Eric. It shows all those days and months ahead of us. It tells the nights when there will be a full moon and a half-moon and the ones with no moon at all. Look, you can

4

see George Washington's birthday in red, in February—and your birthday away off in June! And who knows what will happen before we reach the end of the calendar?"

"Say," Dad put his head in the door, "will you please stop crystal-gazing, madam, and remember I'm a hungry man? I want my dinner."

"Oh, excuse me, dear, of course. Coming right up!" Mother laughed and ran to the kitchen.

Eric was still staring at the calendar.

"What does S - e - c. 3 stand for, Dad?" he asked pointing to some printing on one side of the January page.

"S-e-c. 3? Section three, I suppose, but I don't know what it is there for. Must be a secret," he said. "Secret Three."

Eric's eyes grew larger and his light eyebrows went up higher. Secret Three! Secret Three! The words went over and over in his head as he looked at the snow falling on the calendar. Maybe it was a code. Maybe whoever made that calendar was sending a message to someone. *Secret Three. . . .*

"Come to dinner," called his mother.

Why, he could give one calendar to Tony and

one to Robbie and *they* could be the Secret Three. They could use the calendar for a code. Each day could mean something important like —like—Eric put his finger on January 27th. "J-27"—that could mean "Danger—watch out!"

His Dad's voice reached him. "Eric, will you please come to dinner! *Right this minute!*"

Eric went down the hall to the dining room but he had plans in his head and his thoughts were far away.

A Storm Inside

EARLY THE NEXT MORNING, since it was Saturday, Eric ran across the hall to see his best friend, Tony Felipe. He had the calendar to give him and was anxious to explain all about the Secret Three idea.

Tony and his family had moved to the Hill-dale apartments the same year that the Lees

had. Eric and Tony were only three then and
now they were nine. The boys had been friends
a long time. Their apartments were both on
the first floor of the building: Eric's was No.
11-C and Tony's 12-C.

Eric had no brothers or sisters, so he had a
wonderful time when he went over to the Felipes
where there were five of them: Tony, nine;
Guido, seven; Maria, five; Henri, three; and little Donato, just a year old. Tony, Henri and
Donato had dark wavy hair and black eyes like
their father, but Maria and Guido were light like
their mother. They were almost a second family
to Eric, sort of cousins. And there was always
something exciting going on at their house.

"Come in! Come in!" shouted several voices
when Eric had rung the bell. Before he could
open the door, it swung inward and he was
surrounded by Tony, Maria and Henri. Tony,
his dark hair rumpled and his black eyes bright,
spotted the calendar under Eric's arm.

"What's that, Eric?" he asked, but with so
many Felipes around, Eric didn't want to give
away any secrets. He slipped the parcel to Tony.

"Put this away and I'll tell you about it later,"
he whispered.

Put it away! There was no place in the
Felipes' apartment to put anything away where
little hands could not find it. Just now all the
heavy, beautifully - carved furniture which
Tony's grandmother had brought from Italy was
pushed back against the walls as though for
house cleaning. *Something* was going on, as
usual. Tony quickly stuck the calendar inside
a rolled-up rug.

They pulled Eric into the living room. Mrs.
Felipe was seated at the grand piano. She smiled
at him gaily.

"Hello, Eric! The children are playing snowflakes. Want to watch?"

"Okay." Mrs. Felipe was one of the mothers
Eric liked best. Her light hair had a blow-away
look and her blue eyes twinkled. But Eric liked
her because she was always ready to do things
with her children.

"Come on, Tony, let's finish the storm music,"
she called now. Tony grinned at Eric but once
he sat at the piano his dark face grew tense and
excited.

Softly and slowly at first, then faster and
louder, Tony and his mother began to play.

Eric watched Henri and Maria flinging them-

selves wildly about. Faster and faster, they
circled the room, their arms outflung and their
bodies swaying down to the ground and up
again. It was a fierce storm. The baby crawled
in and out among their legs crowing delightedly.

Then suddenly, Maria, her hair a yellow mist
about her face, tripped dizzily and fell flat on
poor baby Donato!

Such howls and screams as filled the air! All
the Felipes had good lungs and could make
plenty of noise, but Donato seemed to have the

lustiest voice of all. Mrs. Felipe jumped up, took him in her arms and began circling about the room.

"There, there, Di, Di, Dumpling, you are not hurt at all. Shush, now shush!"

But hurt or not, Dumpling continued to howl.

"I guess he's hungry. Here, you hold him, Eric, while I fix his bottle. He likes you. Sit here on the sofa and I'll put him in your lap."

Mrs. Felipe handed the curly-headed baby to Eric carefully. Eric loved to hold him, he was so fat and soft. He stopped crying to look into Eric's face with big eyes and a bubble bursting from his mouth. Henri, who was almost as plump as Donato, climbed upon the sofa beside them.

"Want to sit in your lap, too, Ehwic!" he said pushing close to the baby. Then Maria pushed in on the other side. Tony gave her hair a yank.

"Don't crowd around so," he ordered. "Eric can't breathe."

"I can too," grinned Eric. He was enjoying himself, but he did wonder when he could tell Tony about the Secret Three. There was no place for secrets at the Felipes'.

11

"Let me alone," wailed Maria, striking back at Tony and kicking out with her feet. Fortunately Mrs. Felipe came in just then with the baby's bottle, and Bessie, the maid, followed her from the kitchen to put a plate of doughnuts on the table.

"Now stop your fighting," Bessie warned, shaking her slightly grizzled grey head. "You-all go get Guido and eat those doughnuts and keep quiet!" She rescued little Donato from Eric's lap and there was a scramble for the doughnuts.

"Where's Guido?" Eric asked, a doughnut half filling his mouth.

"Oh, he's in the bedroom making something," answered Tony and the whole crew tore down the hall shouting,

"Guido, Guido! Come get some doughnuts."

The bedroom was full of beds. Baby Donato slept in a crib in the room with his father and mother but the others shared one room. There was a double-decker on one side and two single beds in the center leaving very little space for play. Near the window sat Guido, his head bent over a boat he was laboriously carving. He hardly seemed to hear them. He was a stocky, serious fellow and he loved boats.

"What are you going to do with this piece?" Henri asked.

He reached for a small, thin strip that Guido had been whittling at all morning and suddenly snapped it in two.

Guido looked up in dismay. "Henny!" he cried. "That was my main mast! I worked and worked carving that! Oh, darn, darn, darn. I just can't keep anything around here." He threw his boat down on the carpet beside the broken pieces of his carefully whittled mast.

"Naughty Henny," Maria scolded and began chasing him over the beds.

Eric and Tony stood looking at Guido's boat. Eric liked to construct things, too. But he always had a shelf where he could put unfinished work and know it wouldn't be disturbed. He flung his arm about Guido's shoulder.

"Bring it over to my room, Guido," he said. "You can make your boat there and nobody'll bother it." Guido looked up, brushing his eyes with his sleeve.

"Gee, Eric, can I really? If I just had some place of my own!"

He glanced at his brother and sister still

13

bouncing on the beds and then with Eric's help, gathered up his things.

"Get that package I gave you and come, too, Tony," Eric said. "I've got something important to tell you."

Eric was surprised to see his Dad leaving the apartment as he and Guido and Tony crossed the hall.

"Where are you going, Dad?"

"Just down to the office to make some drawings. See you later."

In the safety of Eric's room Guido was soon busily carving on his boat. There are times, thought Eric, when it is nice to have lots of brothers and sisters, and there are times when it is nice to be alone. After the excitement of the Felipes', having a room all of his own where no one disturbed anything seemed pretty nice.

He and Tony settled on the bed and Eric unrolled the calendar.

"Say, that's neat," exclaimed Tony. "Where'd you get it?"

Eric explained about his Dad bringing the three calendars home and then he pointed to the Sec. 3. "And what do you suppose that means, Tony? Can you guess?"

14

"Search me," Tony shrugged his shoulders. He left all imagining and guessing to Eric.

"It means Secret Three. This whole calendar is secret code, and do you know what, Tony? You and Robbie and I are going to be the Secret Three and use it for signals!"

Tony's eyes flew wide. "Gee, that sounds great! But how can we use a calendar for a code?"

"Well," Eric had given this a lot of thought. "Look, today is January the 21st when we are starting the Secret Three. So whenever you or Robbie or I mean we want to start something we say 'J-21' and nobody knows what we mean but us. Like here's January 27th. We can say 'J-27' and that means 'Danger—watch out!' Every month we'll pick out different signals and nobody'll know what they mean except us three."

"What about me?" asked Guido suddenly lifting his head. "I know what the signals mean. Can I be in the club?"

Eric and Tony looked at one another. They had rather forgotten about Guido who was working over his carving as busily and quietly as an electric clock. But Eric shook his head positively.

"No, you can't be a Secret Three," he said severely. "There can only be three in that! But—" after all Guido knew their secrets so he'd have to be something. Eric looked at the calendar again. "You can be a 31!" he cried at last.

"What's that?" asked Guido.

"Well, that's an 'extra'," answered Eric. "Some months have 31 days instead of 30, so 31 is an extra. You can be an extra. But you have to take an oath first and swear not to tell anything you know."

Guido nodded his head. "I take an oath," he promised.

"Oh, it's not that easy." Eric glanced at Tony. "He's got to do it standing on his head. You take one leg and I'll take the other and we'll hold him upside down while he swears!"

Guido looked startled but decided that anything was worth being an Extra in the Secret Three. So he got on the floor and raised his stocky body in the air. The other two grabbed his legs.

"Say, 'I solemnly swear—',"

"I solemnly swear—" gulped Guido.

"Never to betray any secrets which I have heard."

"Never to betray—" Guido was getting red in the face and having a hard time breathing—"any—secrets—which" gulp "I—have heard . . ."

"That I—"

Mrs. Lee came to the bedroom door. "What on earth!" she cried. "Let Guido down this minute! His face is as red as a sunset!"

Tony and Eric dropped Guido's legs. Mrs. Lee bent over him.

"Are you all right, Guido, child?" she asked.

Guido gulped again. "Sure," he grinned. He looked at Tony and Eric. "Did I make it? Am I a 31?" he asked.

Eric nodded. "It's O.K."

Guido got up and Mrs. Lee, assured that he was all right, went away.

"Come on, Tony," Eric said. "Now we've got to tell Robbie about everything and take him a calendar, too. Don't forget 'J-27'—'Danger—Watch out!' "

Plans for a Shack

Before Eric and Tony set off to explain to Robbie about the calendar, Mrs. Lee called to Eric. She looked at him seriously and said: "Eric, I just want to tell you something. Daddy has not been getting very much work lately. He went to the studio today, but he isn't busy. So, will you please not ask him for presents when he comes home at night?"

Eric started to speak but she held up her hand. "I know, you don't ask for much and the calendars were free, but we mustn't let Daddy feel that it is important to bring something home for us. We want to make him feel we are glad to see him just for himself."

"I am, Mums!" Eric protested. "But, gosh, I just like a present now and then!"

Mrs. Lee did not smile. "You like to go to Fairport, too, don't you?"

Eric's face brightened. Fairport! He *loved* to go to Fairport, the small town by the sea where his family had spent every summer since he could remember. Fairport, where their house had a room in the attic for him, and where he could swim and row a boat and, oh, do a hundred things!

"Of course, I like to go to Fairport!" he cried.

"Well, remember this. The house we have always rented has been sold and we are going to have to find another. It is bound to cost a lot of money and Daddy is doing his best to make it. You know, that depends on how many orders he gets for drawings, and," she glanced at the telephone where Eric knew the pile of letters were all bills, "right now he does not have many orders. We may not even be able to go to Fairport this year."

Eric could only stare at her. Not go to Fairport!

"But we've got to go to Fairport, Mums! We've just got to!"

His mother put her hand on his shoulder. "I know we'll go if Daddy can possibly manage it. Just remember about asking for presents."

"I won't ask for anything. Just so we go to Fairport!"

Eric ran to catch up with Tony. The air was cold and nippy. The black branches of the trees snapped together with a dry, brittle sound and the clouds raced across a slate blue sky.

"Gosh, I wish it would snow!" said Tony, breaking in on Eric's thoughts.

"Me, too," he agreed. He was thinking of his new Christmas sled which he hadn't had a chance to use. It was a Super Racer. Wonder why his Dad hadn't bought him a Flexible Rider? That was the kind all the other kids had.

"Hi, Eric. Where you going?" A girl with dark brown hair flying on her forehead ran to catch up with the boys. It was Debbie Fisher.

"We're going to Robbie's on business," Eric told her, not anxious to have any girls along.

"I'm going to Robbie's, too," said Debbie,

and in order to forestall any objections, added, "his mother invited me."

"Oh, she did, did she?" exclaimed Tony tossing his black curly hair. "Well, you play with his mother then because we've got something very important to talk to Robbie about."

Debbie's brown eyes still looked at Eric and since he didn't say anything more she jogged along quietly behind them, smiling to herself.

"First thing you know she'll want to be an Extra 31," Tony grumbled.

Eric shook his head, glancing sidewise at Debbie, who was listening intently. "No more Extras in January," he said decidedly.

Robbie lived in a house on a nearby street. It had a yard and basement and an attic so there were lots of places where Robbie and his friends could talk and make plans without being interrupted. And Robbie's father and mother always made them feel so welcome, too.

As they came near, they saw Robbie's uncle, the rabbi, just leaving in his car. The first time Eric had met Rabbi Klein, he had felt sure that "Rabbi" meant he was a magician. Mrs. Lee had explained that a rabbi was the same as a minister or a priest, like Rev. Barry at their church and Father John at Tony's. But Eric still had the feeling that Rabbi Klein could do tricks if he wanted to. His dark eyes sparkled at them now.

"You are just in time to see a most remarkable job of scalping," he said. Then he laughed at their puzzled faces.

"Teddy's just given himself a haircut. Go in and see." He waved goodbye and drove away. Teddy was Robbie's young brother.

Eric whistled and Robbie came out of the house. He was a round, chubby boy whose brown eyes were unusually full of fun. But just now he looked a trifle sulky.

"Aw heck," he said. "I've got to take Teddy up to the barber shop. He cut his hair and is it a mess!" Robbie had to grin in spite of himself. Eric and Tony grinned, too. Seems as though every kid does the same thing, thought Eric. He remembered when he and Tony cut theirs. The worst was when they cut Debbie's, though. He glanced at her to see if she remembered. She was smiling so he guessed she did. Boy, was her mother mad!

"Shucks," said Tony," we have some important secrets to tell you. Do you have to go right away?"

"Let's go in the back," he said and they ran around quickly. Sitting on the back steps, Eric handed him his calendar.

"It's all about the Secret Three."

"What's that?" asked Robbie as he unrolled the package.

"You tell him, Tony."

Robbie's eyes looked like round, brown pennies as he listened to the idea of the secret code and signals.

"Say, that's great!" he cried, "and you know what? We ought to have a secret sign, too." He put three fingers on his chubby chin and closed his right eye. "How's this?"

Eric and Tony tried it. "That will be our sign, all right."

"And you know what?" Robbie jumped up and waved his arm. "My Dad said we could have that lumber left over from our garage to build a shack. We could make it a club house for the Secret Three!"

Eric popped up, too, at this suggestion. "A club house! Where could we build it?"

"Right there in the lot next to us. Dad owns a lease on that property. We'd have to cut down some of the little trees but that would be easy."

"Come on, let's get started!"

Robbie's face fell. "I've got to take Teddy to the barber's and I've got to get a haircut, too."

"O.K., then Tony and I'll go along," Eric decided. Tony nodded. "And I'll take some paper and we can draw some plans for the club we are going to build. It's got to have secrets in it. And nobody can come into it but us." He caught sight of Debbie who had just come around the house. She had heard something

25

about building because she said, "I'm good at hammering nails. I could help."

Eric sighed. "O.K., I guess you'll have to be an Extra since you are always around." Eric was exasperated but Debbie grinned happily. "But nobody can be unless they take the oath," objected Tony.

"You're right," Eric agreed. "Bend over, Debbie, and put your head down."

Nothing ever startled Debbie. She did as she was told.

"Now say, 'I solemnly swear never to give away any secrets of the Secret Three until death do us part.'"

"But I don't know any secrets," Debbie protested, bouncing up.

"O.K., say it anyway. If you help build the shack, you'll know some."

"Oh," she smiled and putting her head down again, repeated, "I solemnly swear never, *never* to give away any secrets until death do us part."

"She got off easy," Tony grumbled. "We made Guido stand on his head."

"But I don't know any secrets yet!" Debbie said.

"That's good," grinned Robbie. "Come on, let's go."

Tony, Eric and Robbie with Teddy were soon sitting in Mr. Jensen's sparkling little barber shop. There's something awfully nice about a barber shop, Eric thought. It smelled good, of tonic and shaving stuff, and it looked so clean with the white chairs and the long mirror and Mr. Jensen's pink face with the big mustache pointed at both ends. But the best thing about Mr. Jensen's shop was the three bird cages full of canaries in it. They twittered and hopped from their swinging perches to the wire bars and sang as loudly as they could.

"How much for a canary, Mr. Jensen?" Eric always asked.

"Not for sale. They iss my family, Eric," Mr. Jensen always replied. "Sing, little Jenny Lind, sing Galli and Caruso," he called to the birds and they sang away.

Mr. Jensen's pink face creased into a big smile when he saw Teddy. "Another fellow trying to put me out uff bizness doing hiss own vork," he laughed. "Not much ve can do but gif you a shafe now. Op here, yong fellow."

27

He put Teddy in the automobile which was the seat for small children. I remember when I sat in the automobile, thought Eric. I'm too big for that now. Pretty soon I'll be getting a shave. He looked at the head rest where men put their heads back in comfort while they were lathered by Mr. Jensen. He felt his chin. He couldn't quite believe that whiskers would grow there. One thing for sure, if they did, he was going to have a nice, big mustache with points on it like Mr. Jensen's.

"Come on, Tony and Robbie, let's get busy on the plans," he said. He spread out the piece of paper on the table where the magazines were. "Your house is here, Robbie," Eric drew a square, "and the garage is here," another square, "now where's the best place for the shack?"

Robbie took the pencil and made a square in another spot.

"Right here," he said.

"Mark north on this side and south on this side and east and west," put in Tony, "So it looks regular."

"Sure, that's right," Eric agreed. "But what are we going to have for secrets? Do you think we could make a tunnel underneath it so we

could crawl in and out?"

Mr. Jensen looked over at them beaming. "What you doin'? Goin' to build a shack?" The boys nodded. Mr. Jensen looked around to be sure there wasn't anyone hiding in the small shop. Then he put his scissors down and came over to them.

"In the old country," he whispered, "my brothers and me built a fine shack. Ve had front door for effryone to see but in back was a flap slides back and forth and nobody knows about. Ve all go in front door and slip out back and nobody guess how ve get oudt. Look, I draw you a picture."

Eric, Tony and Robbie watched carefully. "Say, that's a swell secret," they all agreed.

"Think we ought to make Mr. Jensen an Extra?" Robbie whispered.

Eric couldn't see Mr. Jensen standing on his head and swearing their oath. "Better skip it, I guess. But you know what? We all ought to get special haircuts. Crew cuts, I think."

"Crew cuts in the winter time?" asked Tony.

Eric nodded. "That's why they'd be special. Nobody else has crew cuts in the winter time."

However, as it turned out, neither could the Secret Three.

Mr. Jensen shook his head, "Your mothers come up here hopping," he said. " 'Mr. Jensen, ve send boys op for good haircuts. Ve trust you! Look, crew cuts in the vinter time—they all take cold.' No, sir!"

The canaries sang especially loud at this point as though cheering for Mr. Jensen.

But special haircuts or not, the boys were excited about the shack now and could hardly wait to start building. They did not know that their project was going to be delayed for quite a while because of J-27.

"Danger—Watch out!"

The Blizzard

Eric, Tony, Robbie and Debbie were in the Fourth Grade at P.S. 81 and on January 27th, the day Eric called a signal for danger, they were working hard on their arithmetic problems without a thought of J-27.

Eric put his elbows on his desk and looked his problems over carefully again. He rumpled his blond hair and screwed up his eyes. Um-m, he *thought* he had them all right. He rubbed his nose and chewed his pencil. The examples were pretty hard this morning, 'specially that long addition one. It was tough.

He glanced at his teacher, Miss French. Her head with its dark red hair wound in braids on top was bent over a book on her desk. He glanced at Freddie Johnson and Debbie working hard at the blackboard. Heck, how Debbie made her chalk squeak! Wish I could make it squeak like that. It's a wonder Miss French doesn't say something. He looked across the aisle at Robbie. Robbie's chubby forehead was wrinkled and his tongue protruded from the corner of his mouth. He'll never get that long addition one right, thought Eric. Tony's got his, though, and—suddenly Eric stared at the window.

Jim-min-ee Cricket—it was snowing! Hundreds of large flakes had begun to dash across the windows as though they were trying to get inside. They looked like white battalions from another world coming to attack the school. Hundreds of them, thousands of them!

"Oh boy!" Eric exclaimed without realizing that he was almost shouting, "just look at it snow!"

Every head turned toward the windows. Even Miss French, who had started to frown at Eric for shouting, was caught by the excitement of the whirling flakes. The whole fourth grade was standing up now to see, because here it was the end of January and there hadn't been any real snow since Christmas. There were a lot of new sleds besides Eric's which had never been used.

Miss French smiled at the excited faces.

"It does look wonderful," she said. "Hand in your papers and get your hats and coats. It is time for the noon bell."

The school doors opened and the children went bursting into the yard like soda-water from a pop bottle. They shouted and held up their hands to the flying flakes.

"I hope it comes down all day and all night and reaches to the second story windows," cried Eric, grabbing for Tony's cap and turning loose his tangle of black hair.

Tony ducked his head and grabbed for Eric's cap. "So do I," he yelled. "And they have to build tunnels to get out of the houses and school closes up and—"

"We can go coasting all day!" shouted Robbie. "Whoopee!"

Tony rolled on the ground with Robbie and Eric flung himself on top of the pile.

They struggled for a minute and then were up, pushing and scuffling until they came to the corner where Robbie parted from the other two. There was an open field across from the school and Tony and Eric cut through it to reach the Hilldale apartments, rising like a castle on the further edge.

Eric stopped running a minute and lifted his face to the sky.

"Um-m, it's really coming down." The flakes were swirling and dancing so wildly that it made him dizzy to look at them. He felt like flinging himself around as the others had done to Mrs. Felipe's music.

"What if the snowflakes were men from Mars dressed up in white armor?" he asked Tony. "What if they had tiny weapons and were trying to conquer the earth? I'd fight them, wouldn't you? We'd smash them all together, wouldn't we?"

"Sure we would!" Tony tried to catch some right then, swinging about awkwardly so he almost fell down.

Eric closed his eyes and opened his mouth. How cold and tickly the flakes felt on his tongue. He could probably swallow a hundred white soldiers in a minute!

Debbie came trudging up beside them. She had snowflakes on her eyelashes and bangs.

"Look, Eric, I'm Snow White," she said, smiling slowly at him.

"You're Dopey, the dwarf!" cried Eric trying to scrape up enough snow to make into a ball.

Several children passed them. "Hey, you'll be late to lunch," they called.

"You'll be late yourself," Eric answered back, but he and Tony began to race for home. Debbie followed as fast as she could. The boys ran into the apartment house. "Say," said Eric as they were about to turn, each to his own door, "I just happened to think—today's J-27. Remember? 'Danger—watch out!' " He laughed. What could be dangerous about the snow?

Tony laughed, too. "Bye, see you after lunch, Eric."

Eric rushed into his home letting a swish of cold fresh air in with him. It was quiet and peaceful inside. The light from the blustery world outdoors played brightly over the furniture. There was a nice cooking smell which made him feel even hungrier than he thought he was. Chicken noodle soup, he could tell.

"Mums! Mums?" She was sure to be there but he had to *hear* her.

"Here in the kitchen, Eric," answered his mother.

"It's snowing hard." Eric dropped his cap and jacket on the nearest chair. His hair, so nicely plastered down before school, was all awry again. His eyes were bright and cold and his nose and cheeks were pink.

His mother came into the hallway. "Those cheeks look like pink ice cream! May I have a nibble? Um-m, tastes like it, too," she laughed. "Wash your hands, dear, and come eat your lunch."

Eric washed with the least amount of water possible and was soon at the table. "Where's Nana?" he asked. Nana was Eric's grandmother who had come to pay them a visit. She often spent a month or two with the Lees since Grand father Hale had died.

Mother glanced anxiously at the storm outside. "She's down town shopping. I hope she gets home before the streets are too bad."

"What about Daddy? I hope he gets home, too."

"Oh, Daddy's young and strong. He'll get home all right."

"Do you think he'll go sledding with me tomorrow?" Eric asked. Tomorrow was Saturday.

Mother nodded. "If he doesn't have to work." There was a little frown between her eyes. She looked at Eric. "He is trying to design a new calendar. It might mean we can go to Fairport if it turns out well."

If it turns out well. Eric didn't like that *if*, or the worried look on his mother's face. There shouldn't be any "if" about Fairport. He couldn't help scowling.

His mother glanced at the clock.

"Now, you'd better be getting back to school. If you get snow-bound, I'll send a dog team for you. And wear your boots."

Eric's face grew darker. "My boots? Gosh, Mums, I don't need those old things." He flung on his jacket and cap, preparing to dash.

"Wear your boots," Mrs. Lee repeated firmly.

Reluctantly, Eric fished in the closet and pulled the hated galoshes on, mumbling to himself. His mother smiled and at last he had to smile back. He gave her a quick kiss.

"Bye," he grinned. The door slammed behind him and he ran across the hall. Tony was ready to leave.

"I had to wear boots," Eric said.

"Sh,—my mother forgot mine," Tony warned, putting a finger to his lips, his black eyes shining. There were so many children in Tony's family that it was hard for his mother to keep an eye on them all. "The radio says 'the storm may reach blizzard proportions,'" he added excitedly.

39

"J-27 Danger—watch out!" cried Eric.

Already a coat of white velvet covered the ground and lay like Christmas trimmings on the bare black branches of the trees.

"It looks like the Far North," Eric said. "We won't be able to work on the shack now for a while. Look, I'm King of the Royal Mounted and you're a crook escaped from jail. I'm after you with my dog team. Mush, mush, you huskies, mush!"

The two boys ran through the field, and Eric, with his arms outstretched to catch snowflakes on his jacket, bumped into Debbie.

"You are my prisoner! You can't escape now. Get on this sled. I'm taking you back to jail along with Crooked Jack, here," he told her.

"O.K., Eric, only I don't see any sled."

Robbie caught up with the group. "Gee, it's ten to. We better hurry," he called to them.

They reached the school yard just as their line was disappearing into the building. Dick Higgins, the monitor, a tall, thin boy with merry eyes behind glasses, made a face at them. "I ought to report you," he warned. He turned to Debbie who was still walking very slowly.

"You hurry, Debbie Fisher, or you are going to be marked late."

Debbie just smiled at him and went her own sweet way to class.

The snow beat on the windows all afternoon. None of the children could get their minds on anything else. Miss French told her class that they were going to give a play about George Washington at Valley Forge, so this would be a good time to start practicing for it. She chose Tony for General Washington and then looked at Eric. Eric shrank into his seat. He liked to pretend and to play things but not in front of all the rest of the school in Assembly hall. Before Miss French could make up her mind to call him, he put up his hand.

"Miss French, could I be the announcer or the stage manager, or something?" he asked.

Miss French hesitated a minute but his eyes implored her. "Very well, Eric, you can be the stage manager *and* the announcer."

Eric sat down with relief. That part would be fun.

When school was dismissed for the day, Eric and Tony found the snow almost a foot deep.

It was still falling but not softly now. It was half ice. The wind was bitter cold and the boys had to fight to make headway. Cars parked along the street looked like igloos, and traffic was moving very slowly.

Debbie had her small sister, Bridget, by the hand. She called to Eric.

"We can hardly see," she cried.

Robbie shouted at Eric and Tony. "Secret Three to the rescue! J-27. We'll form a line and you two walk behind us and hold onto our coats," he told Debbie and Bridget. "We'll go home by the sidewalk instead of through the field."

They were all huffing and puffing when they

reached the buildings. Many mothers were rushing through the storm to bring the younger children home. Eric, Tony and Robbie went back several times to form a windbreak for the smallest ones.

That old calendar knew this was going to happen all along, Eric thought. I hope Nana and Daddy are home. He shook off as much of the snow as possible before he entered the apartment.

Nana was there bustling about like a disturbed hen. She was a plump little woman with a pile of lovely grey hair and a vast amount of energy. She hugged and kissed Eric hard. "I'm glad you got home, Nana," he said.

43

"Well, I'm surely glad to see you safely here, too," she cried. "Get those wet things off at once and I'll hang them in the bathroom with mine. Did I have a time! I thought the wind would knock me down. I wish your Daddy had sense enough to come before things get any worse."

Eric heard his mother's voice. She was talking over the phone to Dad. "You'll have trouble getting up from the station even now, dear," she said, "and the radio says train schedules are upset, too. It's a real blizzard."

She listened to his voice with a crease between her eyes. Then she shook her head. "Well, come as soon as you can." She put down the receiver and looked at Eric. "He has a small job he just has to finish," she explained, but something in her eyes made Eric feel uneasy. I wish he would come home, he thought.

By this time the storm was much too bad for the children to play outside. The space they had cleared for the Secret Three club house was deep under the snow. So Eric decided to go over to see if Tony's father had come home. It was not long before Mr. Felipe did come home, bursting into the apartment like a sky rocket, shaking snow like sparks all over the room.

He was a tall angular man with a shock of black curly hair and bright black eyes like his boys'. The children rushed to him shrieking, "Papa! Papa! What did you bring us?" Just like me, thought Eric.

"Great worshipful saints and little curly-headed angels!" replied Mr. Felipe. "It's lucky I brought *myself* in one piece. Mama mia! This is the most utterly fantastic storm I ever fell up and down in!" He swept off his hat and coat with wide gestures. Mrs. Felipe caught them before they fell to the floor. "You, children, be thankful to see your papa this night. The trains are running like snails. The buses have stopped. The hill up from the station is insurmountable. It is a great wonder I have reached here at all!" He sank dramatically upon the sofa.

Mrs. Felipe caught sight of Eric's anxious face.

"Come now, Vincent," she said in a warning voice, "It can't be quite as bad as that. I think you are play-acting a little for fun. After all, other fathers beside you are managing to get home."

Mr. Felipe waved his hands. "Perhaps they are home even now," he said, smiling gaily.

Eric ran quickly across the hall. But his Dad had not come. Mother was calling the studio to tell him that the buses had stopped running. There was no answer to the ringing phone. "At least he's left. He may be here any minute now," she said.

"He's more likely cooped up on a stalled train halfway between here and the city," Nana said gloomily.

Eric stood watching from the window. It had grown dark outside and still the white battalions hurled themselves down. It looked as though they were trying to smother the world, bury it with their glistening army. And I was the one who wanted it to come up to the second-story windows, thought Eric. O.K., let it—but not before Daddy gets home. What good is the Secret Three now? We can't make a windbreak for Dad. But if I knew where he was, I'd try.

"WARNING TO ALL MOTORISTS," said a voice on the radio, "ROADS OUT OF THE CITY ARE IMPASSABLE. THE SUDDEN AND UNPREDICTED BLIZZARD HAS TEMPORARILY SWAMPED THE SNOW-CLEARING EQUIPMENT. TRAINS ARE ONE AND

TWO HOURS BEHIND SCHEDULE. BUSES ARE NOT RUNNING IN SOME AREAS—" Mother turned the announcement off.

"Come and eat your dinner, Nana and Eric. I'll put Dad's over some hot water to keep it warm. Sounds as though he'll have a time getting here. But I bet a cookie he'll be here soon."

Mother, Nana and Eric sat down to dinner. It wasn't strange that none of them were very hungry. Even Nana's "Keep your fingers out of your plate, Eric. Take your elbow off the table!" did not have much pep to them. She finally said loudly, "Well, *if* he has fallen and broken a leg on the ice, some one will find him and let us know, I'm sure."

Mother had to laugh. "Oh, my goodness, Nana! It's probably just as you said. He's most likely sitting on the train somewhere between stations reading his paper and mad as hops."

Dinner was over and the dishes washed and still no Dad. Then, suddenly, they heard someone at the door. Eric rushed to open it. And there he was. His face was pale and drawn with cold. There was no sign of the usual broad grin on his mouth or twinkle in his eyes. He stumbled as he entered the hall. Mother put

47

an arm around him and helped him to a chair. His clothes were stiff with coated ice. Nana quickly brought a steaming drink and Mother held it to his lips.

"Run, fill the tub with hot water, Eric," she said. He was glad of something to do. He had never seen his father look like that before.

At last, Dad was able to smile a little. "I don't think any of me's frozen," he told them, "but

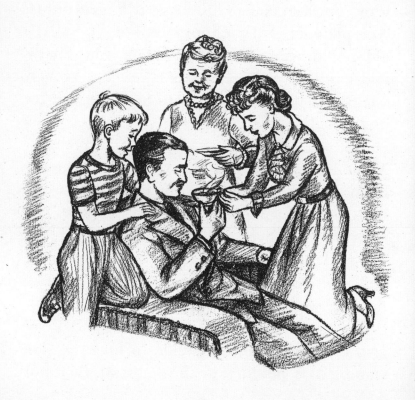

man, oh man, am I tired! I couldn't phone you," he looked apologetically at mother, "though I knew you'd be worried, because when I got off the subway and found there were no buses or taxis running, I headed for the parkway thinking the walking would be easier. But it wasn't. It was awful—drifts of ice and snow to my knees. It must be two miles there on that parkway with not a store or anything to stop into. I should have taken a chance on the trains. At least the hill would have been shorter." He glanced around at Eric. "Guess I wouldn't be much good as a Royal Mountie!"

Eric put his arm about his father's neck. "You ought to have called the Secret Three, Dad. We could have brought a dog team!"

"Danger—watch out." That old calendar knew a thing or two. What would its days bring next?

A Battle and a Wounded Soldier

As SOON AS ERIC WOKE UP the next morning, he hopped out of bed and ran to the window to see the snow. It was eight o'clock—he had slept much later than he meant to—and the sun was blazing down on a brilliant white world. The snow did not rise to the second story windows but it was at least three feet deep and there were drifts that rose much higher where the wind had blown. It was the trees and bushes, however, which made the whole out-doors look like an enchanted fairyland. Every branch to the tiniest twig was coated with ice as sparkling as Cinderella's glass slipper. And overhead the sky was a bright, clear blue.

"Gee whiz!" whispered Eric to himself. And then he ran to see if his mother had looked out upon the shining scene.

"It really is wonderful," she agreed. "I feel as though we had waked up inside Aladdin's cave of jewels."

Eric nodded. "And they are all diamonds!" he added.

He was not content long just to look. "Dress quietly," mother warned, "Dad's still sleeping."

Eric went back to his room and looked at his calendar. J-27 was already marked with a red circle and now he put a red X over J-28. That's for Xciting, he thought. Today is going to be Xciting! In record time he threw on his clothes and dashed from the house. Tony and Guido and Maria were already making "angels" by falling flat in the drifts and Eric had soon made his share. And then they began pelting each other with snowballs. Other children were dragging their sleds off to the field. "Come on help pack down some slides with us, Eric," they urged. Tony went to get his sled but Eric kept running into the house to see if his dad was awake yet.

"For goodness sakes, either stay in or stay out," urged his grandmother. "You are tracking snow all over the place. Letty," she asked mother, "when do you think Don will be getting up? The biscuits are almost done."

"I'll see," mother answered. "Eric, shake yourself off and put your galoshes in the kitchen. Breakfast is about ready." She tiptoed down the hall. Eric followed close behind her. Dad's eyes flew open when he heard them.

"How do you feel, dear?" asked mother.

"Hungry enough to eat an elephant!" said Dad, grinning and stretching.

"Get ready then," said Mother smiling, "and I'll go and slice one up."

Eric popped into the room. "Dad, it's grand out! The kids are already sliding down the bumps in the field and the snow packs fine. Will you come with me after breakfast?"

"Give me time! Give me time!" begged his father, getting out of bed. "O-o-o! Am I stiff in my joints! Have you tried out your new sled yet?"

"No," answered Eric. "I'm waiting for you." He hesitated a moment and then asked. "Dad, why didn't I get a Flexible Rider?" He cleared his throat. "I'm sure if you picked a Super Racer, it's a good sled, Dad. I only wondered. Most all the kids have Flexible Riders."

Dad looked startled. "A Super Racer? Oh, yes, now I remember. I looked at the two models and it seemed to me the Super had better lines and would be easier to steer. Say, I'll have to hustle and see if I'm right."

The two of them wolfed down the hot biscuits Nana had added to Mother's sausage and scrambled eggs. Mother insisted the sausage was sliced elephant trunk! Then Dad and Eric bundled up. They pulled the sled from the back of a closet where it had stood since Christmas.

"It's a Super, all right," said Dad, kissing Mother goodbye, "and we are going to prove it. Want to come?"

Mother shook her head. "I'd like to but I think after I've straightened up, Nana and I had better go down to the store and see what we can get in the way of groceries. The roads are still not cleared and it may be some time before any deliveries can be made. If we are late getting back, there are lots of wienies and baked beans. Fix yourselves some lunch. Eric may have to haul our things home on his sled later."

Outside, Eric and his Dad joined other boys and girls heading for the field. Some were with their fathers, too, and some with their mothers.

"Hi, Eric," hailed Dick Higgins. "Got a new sled? Is it a Flexible Rider?"

Eric glanced at Dad. "No, it's a Super Racer."

"Um-m," Dick looked at his own sled. It was a Flexible Rider.

Debbie came dragging her sled slowly along. "Hi, Eric. Got a new Flexible Rider?"

"Nope," Eric answered shortly. "Mine's a Super Racer. It's got better lines and steers easier. Can't you see?"

Debbie looked at her own Flexible Rider. "Can I have a ride on yours, Eric?" she asked.

"Sure, I'll let you. But first my father and I have to try it out."

Dad was anxious. He hoped he hadn't made a mistake. That Super Racer had better be good!

They were soon at the top of the nearby hill

which sloped downward for a full block before a stone wall separated it from the street. Grown-ups and children of all ages were already there coasting and Eric saw Tony and Guido trudging back to the top again after their ride. Mr. Felipe waved to them. He had little Donato, warmly bundled, in a box fastened to a sled. "So you are none the worse for your strenuous trip home, I am glad to see!" he said to Mr. Lee. "An amazing storm, perfectly fantastic!"

"It surely was!" Dad laughed.

"Look at me, papa," cried chubby Henri, and he flung himself past them down one of the smaller runs.

"Well, what are we waiting for?" asked Eric's Dad. He placed the Super Racer at the beginning of a track which looked steep and thrilling.

"That one's got a big bump in it halfway down," warned Robbie, who had just come up the hill.

"Thanks, we'll watch for it," promised Mr. Lee. "Sit in front, Eric, and I'll put my legs around you and steer. Give us a push, Robbie. Hi, yi! Here we go!" he cried.

They were off like an icicle sliding down a roof. Swish, swirr, went the sled, up over the bump, down around a curve and slower, slower —almost to the stone fence. Eric's face was glowing.

"Say, that was neat!" Tony yelled at them. "What you got—a Flexible Rider?"

"No, mine's a Super Racer," Eric said with pride. "Steers better, I think."

Tony grinned. "Mine's a Super, too," he admitted. "They are neat." He made the sign of the Secret Three and Eric laughed.

Dad breathed with relief. He hadn't made a mistake after all.

Eric went down the hill several times again, belly whopper alone, and sitting up with Debbie hanging on his back. When he and Debbie climbed up again, he caught sight of a boy from his class, Freddie Johnson, who lived at the orphanage for colored boys. He didn't have a sled.

"Hi, Freddie, what you doing here?" Eric called.

Freddie's white teeth flashed. "I was over at school and saw you kids sliding so I came to watch."

"Want a ride?" asked Eric. "The hill's good."

"Sure!" Freddie came forward smiling all

over. "Thanks, Eric," he cried and he swung himself onto the sled and raced down the hill. Dad was smiling at Eric, too.

"Well, I guess everything is under control," he said. "I'm going in the house and have another cup of hot coffee. See you later!"

"See you later, Dad." Eric waved goodbye and piled on the back of Tony's sled for a slide. When they reached the bottom they noticed that some of the bigger boys were building a fort on one side of the field.

"Say, let's build a fort, too," suggested Tony, "and have a fight with them!"

"Say, that's a good idea. I'll go get our gang and we'll give 'em a real battle! The Secret Three against the Big Guys," cried Eric. He was soon back with Robbie, Freddie, Dick and Guido. Robbie pointed to a spot. "Let's start to build over there," he said. "That part's higher than their territory and we can sail our ammunition right down on them!"

All the boys joined the fort building with enthusiasm and when the bigger boys saw they were going to have enemies they worked harder than ever. Eric rolled a small ball across the fresh snow and it rapidly gathered up carpets of additional snow. His snowball was soon so large he had to call Tony to help him push it into place. J-28—X for Xciting. It sure is, he thought.

"It's wonderful snow for building," Eric said. "We can make a wall with towers on it at both ends in no time." The cold air nipped his cheeks and made him stamp his feet to keep them warm but he was so busy that he didn't mind. Freddie seemed a little chilly, though. He was making ammunition as fast as he could. He looked at Eric and grinned. "We'll fix 'em, won't we, Eric? Shall I stack these cannon balls up in piles?"

"That's swell," said Eric. "Don't you have any gloves, Freddie?"

"I got 'em but they're so wet I stuck 'em in my pocket. My hands ain't cold!"

The fort was hardly shaped before the first warning ball came flying over from the enemy camp.

"Get set, you rebels, you! We're going to attack," cried Billy Henski, captain of the big boys.

"We ain't rebels. We're the Americans!" cried Freddie sticking his head over the top of

the wall and getting a barrage down his neck for his trouble.

"You tell 'em!" yelled Eric and Tony, and the fight was on. Guido ignored everything else except keeping the pile of cannon balls high. He sat calmly behind the wall while the others were throwing and receiving snowballs right and left. Robbie could throw the best of any of them, though Tony was pretty good, too. Dick couldn't throw worth a cent, but he was laughing a lot. Eric and Freddie were so excited that they raced up and down the top of the wall yelling, half the time forgetting to fire anything themselves. Suddenly a hard shot hit Freddie and he slipped. He fell against Eric and they both crashed down behind the fort, Freddie's feet against Eric's forehead. He was up in a minute, helping Eric.

"Gosh, I didn't mean to fall on you. Are you hurt?" Freddie asked anxiously. Eric sat up. He felt a bit dazed. Freddie's shoes were like iron and they *had* hurt.

"It's all right. I'm O.K." he said. But he put his hand to his forehead and found it was bleeding.

"Say, what's the matter, Eric?" The other

boys crowded around. The snow was showing red drops.

"Guess I better go get a Band Aid," Eric said. Gosh, he thought, I hope I don't have to go to the doctor and have stitches or chloroform or anything! Or iodine! He winced at the idea. The other boys yelled for a truce and Billy came over.

"Do you surrender?" he asked. Then he saw Eric. "Say, who did that? Our snowballs weren't that hard!"

"Freddie's shoes did it," Dick said.

Freddie looked miserable. "I didn't mean to."

" 'Course, he didn't," Eric stood up. "Come on, Freddie, it's not so bad. Come along while I put a Band Aid on." He took Freddie's arm and they started up the hill. The others followed them to the Lees' apartment. They were all covered with snow and some of it was reddened with Eric's blood. They looked like veterans who had been in a real battle!

"Mums? Mums!" Eric called as they pushed into the apartment.

A Winter Picnic

DAD WAS SITTING in the living room reading the paper he had brought home the night before, when Eric and his snowy gang burst in.

"Mums! Where's Mums?" Eric asked.

"Mother and Nana went to get some groceries," Dad said and then he noticed Eric's forehead. "Hey, what happened?" He hopped up quickly and came to see.

"We were having a snow fight with the big

boys," said Robbie, "and Freddie jumped on him with both feet."

"Hard, too," Tony added. Freddie was embarrassed.

"He didn't jump," Eric cried hotly. "He just slipped and fell on me."

"I'm sure he didn't mean to hurt you," Dad said. "Let's go to the bathroom and render some First Aid. I guess you can't have battles without casualties!"

They all traipsed down the hall, the snow sliding off their clothes and making puddles on the rug. Five pairs of eyes watched solemnly as Eric's Dad rummaged in the medicine closet.

"Do you have to put iodine on it?" asked Eric anxiously.

Mother would use iodine, Dad thought. Now I wonder if there isn't something else just as good.

"First, I'll swab it off with this clean cotton," his father said, "then"—his eyes ranged the shelves—"maybe a little Mercurochrome would do the job." He heard an audible sigh behind him. That wouldn't hurt!

He soon had Eric swabbed and covered with at least six Band Aids. He really appeared to be a wounded soldier.

"I think he'll live, but I guess he's on the casualty list until after lunch."

"Shucks, we were having so much fun. I wish it didn't have to be over so soon." Eric looked around at his friends' faces.

"Dad," he asked, "could we have a picnic?" Dad's eyes flew wide open and his forehead wrinkled up.

"A picnic in all this snow?" he asked, surprised by such a notion.

"I mean in my room," Eric explained waving his arm. "Mums said there were lots of wienies and baked beans. We could cook 'em and eat on the floor in my room, like a picnic!"

The other boys' faces had brightened excitedly and all were watching Mr. Lee for an answer. Dad rubbed his chin.

"What would your mother say to such an idea?" he asked dubiously.

"Oh, she wouldn't mind, I know!" cried Eric.

"We could put papers on the floor to keep it clean," suggested Guido practically, his blue eyes hopeful.

"And I could bring lots of milk from our

house," Tony offered. "We always have lots of milk."

"Well," Dad weakened slowly, "talk to your mothers. I guess it will be all right—" before the words were fairly out of his mouth there were shouts and everyone began scrambling to do something. Tony rushed across the hall for milk, and Robbie called his mother on the phone to tell her. Eric and Guido and Freddie piled their wet coats in the bathroom, then Guido and Freddie began to spread newspapers on the floor in Eric's room. It seemed such a good idea that they continued the job right down the hall to mop up the puddles which were already there. Eric and Dad went to work in the kitchen, opening the cans of baked beans and putting the wienies on to boil.

Eric flashed a smile into his Dad's face. "Gee, this is swell! This is almost as good as the battle."

"Come and get it!" shouted Dad when the wienies were done. He had fished out some paper plates and cups left from summer picnics and he handed one each to the eager boys. Then he ladled out the beans and put two wienies and a bun on each plate. Eric beamed.

"You know what?" he said. "This is like we were cowboys out on the plains. We been rounding up cattle and now we're camping for the night. You're the 'cookie,' Dad," he grinned, "and this is the chuck wagon."

" 'Ray for the cookie," cried the other boys and Dad sang, "Home on the Range!"

The snow outside faded away and the plains stretched all around them as they settled about the fire which Guido pretended to build in the center of Eric's room. Everybody was busy eating and saying nothing for a few minutes.

"This reminds me of the times when I used to go rabbit hunting with my old dog Troy," Eric's Dad murmured, looking around.

"What kind of a dog was Troy, Mr. Lee?" asked Tony.

"A big white bulldog," answered Eric, who had heard about Troy many times.

"Yes, sir, the best dog in our town," Dad said, "but he couldn't catch rabbits. We boys would take him out to the fields when we went on picnics like this and, pretty soon, up would pop a rabbit."

"An ole jack rabbit, I bet," grinned Freddie.

"Yes, sir, a wise, old jack," agreed Dad. "And Mister Troy would start after him like a bomber chasing a fighting plane. Away goes Mr. Rabbit and away goes Troy, lickety-split. Then, suddenly, that smart jack turns in his tracks and goes off at an angle. Poor, old Troy! He's traveling so fast, he can't switch to save him. He puts on the brakes and bump, bump, bump, he drags his tail feathers on the ground 'til he comes to a stop! Mr. Rabbit is waiting for him, so off Troy goes again as fast as he can travel. When they are both tearing along in fine shape again—Mr. Rabbit turns another corner. Bump, bump, bump, poor Troy puts on the brakes!"

The boys were all laughing at the vision of old Troy trying to catch a rabbit. Dad was grinning, too.

"We had to call Troy back and take him home before long. He was game to go on as long as rabbits popped up, but our insides hurt so from laughing and we didn't want the old dog to wear himself out. Though sometimes he looked as though he knew what the game was and enjoyed it, too. But I'll bet he wished he could catch a rabbit—just once!"

"Troy must have been a fine dog, Mr. Lee," said Robbie.

"He sure was," Eric piped up. "He couldn't catch rabbits, but he could catch rats, couldn't he, Dad?"

Mr. Lee nodded, smiling. Every boy there would wish he had a white bulldog like Troy. Better change the subject, he thought.

"This would be a regular camp if we only had some music," Dad said.

Freddie's eyes shone. "I got a harmonica," he offered shyly, and pulling it from his pocket looked around for encouragement.

"Go ahead and play it, Freddie," cried the boys.

Freddie wiped off the instrument with his sleeve and, rather embarrassed at first, began to play, "Home on the Range."

"Gee whiz, can he play!" whispered Tony to Eric.

Soon they were all singing and clapping to the rhythm. Then Freddie got excited and stepped into the middle of the floor. He played "Turkey in the Straw" and danced to it while the others clapped hands. Finally he turned a

complete somersault without putting his hands to the floor. How the boys shouted at that!

They were having so much fun and making so much noise that no one heard Mrs. Lee and Nana come in.

"Goodness, gracious, sakes alive!" cried Nana when she saw all the newspapers down the hall. "What's going on here?" She and mother followed the messy trail to Eric's room, not overlooking the state of the kitchen, the bathroom and the picnic, itself. However, it was such a gay party that all Mrs. Lee had the heart to say was:

"I hope you left something for us to eat! I knew we had company when I saw all those sleds stacked in the hall."

The boys paused and looked at each other. They had completely forgotten their sleds. The last they had seen of them they were piled behind the snow fort.

"Billy and the big boys must have brought them home. That was pretty swell of them," cried Eric.

"They were sorry you got hurt," Tony put in.

Eric raised his hand to his head. He had even forgotten about his cut.

The boys soon gathered their things together and shouting, "Thanks, Mr. Lee, for the swell picnic," said goodbye and left. Only Robbie and Tony stayed behind for a moment.

"What're the signals for next month, Eric?" they asked.

Eric looked at the calendar. He was going to keep this calendar always—even when he grew old—because its days meant something now. Lincoln's and Washington's birthdays were marked in red on the February page.

"Let's make 'F-12'—that's Lincoln's birthday—stand for 'Strong,'" he said, "and 'F-21,' that's the day we have our old play, stand for 'Awful,' and Washington's birthday 'F-22,' that will mean 'Brave.'"

"You know," Eric added, thinking out loud, "let's make Freddie an Extra 31. He could stand on his head without us holding up his feet!"

"Or even touching the ground," Tony laughed, and Robbie's chubby cheeks wrinkled up. They put three fingers on their chins and winked their right eyes—their secret sign. Then they said goodbye for the day.

"F-22" Brave

ERIC, TONY AND ROBBIE had looked forward to their holiday on George Washington's birthday, and had hoped to get to work on their club house. Now it had arrived but it was a miserable day.

The morning had not been so bad but by noon it had begun to rain and sleet. The rain would let up every little while and they would think it was going to clear, then down it would pour again until everything outdoors was slushy and dripping.

What could you do on a holiday with rain pouring down as though from a fire hose! It couldn't have been more disappointing. "F-22—Brave." What was brave about a day like this?

Tony, Guido and Debby were spending the afternoon with Eric in his room. Robbie was home because he had the beginning of a cold. Eric and Guido's heads were bent over the table where Eric had become absorbed in the model of a house which the Lees had rented so many summers in Fairport—the house which, unhappily, had been sold. Eric had been to the Hobby Shop and bought some smooth, clean strips of balsa wood, some airplane glue, and with the set of sharp blades Tony had given him for Christmas he was determined to make every house he could remember in Fairport. He was going to make a model of the Old Mill, Captain Adams' Clam House, the Harris' red barn, the two bridges—everything. He had a board on which he had painted a grey road, blue water and green grass and he was going to set his models on it so that he could remember all about Fairport even if he couldn't go there.

His face was screwed up with concentration. The porch goes on this side, he was thinking as he cut a small rectangle for a roof. Surely we'll be able to go again! Here's where I slid down from my room the time I was playing Indians with Charley and then I hid in the tall grass of the fields behind the house so long he had to give me up. What fun we had at Fairport. We just must go! He smiled to himself as he glued on the roof. Airplane glue is wonderful the way it sticks, he thought.

Guido was working on another boat, a four-master this time. This was going to be strong enough to go around the world—far away from Henny and Maria—where they couldn't reach it. But, of course, he'd bring them presents when he came sailing home.

Tony and Debby were propped on the studio bed reading. Debby could read forever. You could speak to her — shout at her even — she would never hear you. She was deep in the adventures of Pinocchio. Tony was different; even Roy Rogers' narrow escape in Death Valley could not hold him long. He threw his book down.

"Come on, Eric, let's play guns. Let's build

a fort with pillows and a blanket over the table like we did the other day. You and I on one side and Debby and Guido on the other."

"No fair," Guido said without looking up. "You're both bigger than we are."

"All right, I'll fight the three of you then," Tony rumpled his black hair and came to look over Eric's shoulder. "What you making?"

"Oh darn," Eric threw down a sliver of balsa. He had just cut the support for the porch too short. "It's a house, can't you see? It's a house like the one we had in Fairport. I'm going to make a model of Fairport if it takes me two years!"

Tony's dark eyes showed approval. "It's good, Eric. It looks like a neat house. We are going to get a house, too. I heard Papa talking to Mama last night. He's looking for a house for us down on Long Island!"

Eric stared at his friend. "You mean you'd move away from Hilldale?" But Tony couldn't do that! The Felipes had lived in No. 12 as long as Eric had lived in No. 11. They were almost like his own family. They just couldn't move away. But Tony kept on talking.

"Papa said he wanted a big house where each

76

of us could have our own room, and a basement to play in—"

"Our own room?" Guido looked up. "With a lock for the door?"

Tony nodded. "Sure, I guess so. And we could have a dog—" he noticed Eric's face "and you could come and visit us, Eric, and stay as long as you wanted. You could sleep in my room."

"No, mine!" cried Guido.

Eric put away his construction. He had lost interest in houses. Visiting. That wasn't like running across the hall every day and having the Felipes in his room playing the rest of the time. That was entirely different.

"Come on, Guido, let's play guns. Put your stuff up here." Guido was still in a dream of his own room with a lock and key! "Do you want to play, Debbie? DEBBIE, DO YOU WANT TO PLAY?" Debbie's dark head didn't move. Pinocchio's nose was growing longer and longer as he told a bigger and bigger fib. "Oh, all right," Eric gave up. "Just you and me, then, Tony. But listen, if I get the draw on you, you have to drop. You can't go on shooting, hear?"

"You, too," Tony returned.

The noise of guns firing Br-r-r-rat! Br-r-r-rat! was soon terrific. It was even too much for Pinocchio, so reluctantly Debbie left him. She and Guido joined the ambushing.

But Eric wasn't having as much fun as usual playing guns. He suddenly began feeling unhappy inside. No Fairport, no Felipes, a dog for Tony and none for him. He fired wildly and angrily and often refused to fall when he was fairly shot. The room was in an uproar, finally bringing both Eric's mother and grandmother to the door.

"My goodness, what a racket! We can't hear ourselves think!" cried Nana.

"Eric! Eric! You all will have to quiet down," his mother protested.

Eric, his face flushed and angry, was refusing to be dead, although both Tony and Guido insisted they had "got" him.

"The rain has let up for the time being," said Mrs. Lee. "How would you like to go to the store and get a can of corn to pop?"

"Do I have to wear my rubbers?" Eric stared at her with anger, too, hardly knowing why he was so mad at everyone.

"I'm afraid so. It's so slushy," began his mother.

"Then I won't go!" Eric stormed.

"I'll go," offered Tony, willingly.

"I'll help you put the old rubbers on, Eric, and you go, too," his mother smiled gently at him. "No rubbers, no popcorn."

"F-22," Tony said to him. "Come on, F-22." He gave the secret sign.

Brave, thought Eric. What's brave about rubbers? Maybe he means it's brave to do something you don't want to do.

"Oh, all right. Gimme the old things," and poking his feet into them he glowered at Tony. "So it's F-22 huh? Well, let's go."

"F-23" Wonderful

Eric was still tight and unhappy inside as he and Tony set off for the store. The cool fresh dampness of the air struck them pleasantly. Eric splashed in slush so that it came up over the top of his rubbers and somehow he felt better. But he began to be a little ashamed of himself. I am acting like a baby, he thought. He turned to Tony.

"You probably won't move right away, will you, Tony?" he asked anxiously.

"I don't think so," Tony answered. "My father only started looking, and houses are hard to find these days."

"What kind of a dog would you get, do you 'spose?"

"Um, I don't know." Tony rolled his black eyes, thinking of the endless possibilities. White dogs, black dogs, black and white, brown—airdales, police, scotties, bull dogs! My, what a lot there were to choose from. Perhaps a white bulldog like Troy.

"Say," cried Eric, "What's that dog over there barking at?"

They were passing the school building near which a number of bushes were planted. Their wet black branches were decorated now by silver drops of rain. Around one bush a mean-faced black and tan dog was prancing and yapping. A thin boy with a red nose in his pale face and a stocky boy with a lot of freckles were yelling,

"Sic 'em, Spot! Sic 'em, boy!"

"That's Ed and Harry Pully and their dog, Spot," said Tony. "They're the meanest boys in the fifth grade." Tony pushed back his cap.

81

Eric was interested in seeing what was in the bush. "What are they after?"

He went closer to find out and from the bare, twisted branches two large golden-green eyes stared at him.

"Meow!" cried a plaintive little voice.

"Why, it's a kitty," exclaimed Eric, "and she's scared to death. Get away from here, Spot. Get away!"

"Who you telling to get away?" asked Ed, thrusting his freckled face forward and strutting up belligerently. "You leave our dog alone!"

"Yeah," added Harry, sidling up, too, and pushing his face close to Eric's. "You leave our dog alone."

Tony moved in on the group but Eric didn't give him a chance to get started. "Who's hurting your old dog?" he asked. "Your old dog is scaring that kitty 'most to death."

"Scared to death, is she? That's a laugh! Look at the scratch she gave Spot right across his nose." Harry pointed to the dog and Spot whimpered, to prove he was hurt.

"She scratched him 'cause he scared her! Get away, you old Spot!" yelled Eric.

The yellow dog, deciding he had had enough

of combat for the time, turned tail and ran. But Ed and Harry did not. They were bigger than Eric although Tony was almost their match.

"Don't you treat our dog like that!" cried Ed and he swung his fist into Eric's face. Like a flash, Eric swung back at him. Then Tony and Harry hit each other, and in a second, all four boys were down on the ground in the mud, arms and legs flailing the air.

Tony was managing all right with Harry, but Eric was having a hard time. Ed had a grip on his hair and was banging his head on the ground. The place where he had been hurt in the snow fight began to bleed again. Then he heard a shout and something like a dark cannon ball shot into Ed's stomach. Ed let go with a cry, and Eric sat up to see Freddie, his fists going like hammers, pummeling his opponent. This new assault was more than the Pully boys had bargained for. They scrambled to their feet and took to their heels, yelling, "You just wait! We'll get even with you!"

Tony and Freddie helped Eric up. "Gee. thanks, Freddie, you came in the nick of time!"

"What's all the trouble 'bout?" asked Freddie as Eric felt his head. He and Tony were muddy messes, but the first thing he thought of was the cat.

"I'm trying to get that poor little kitty in the bushes there. The Pully boys' dog Spot scared her to death." He reached carefully toward the little animal. "Here, Kitty! Here, kitty!"

"Mer-row." The big eyes flashed and the cat shrank against the branches.

"Are you goin' to try to pick her up, Eric?" asked Freddie.

"Sure, she won't hurt me if she knows I won't hurt her. I'm going to take her home and give her some milk. Nice, kitty. Nice, kitty!" Eric stretched his hand gently into the bush. He felt the wet head and stroked it.

"Meow," the cat cried softly, "Meow, meow." As easily as he could, Eric detached the small trembling body from the branches and cuddled it in his arms. He did get a scratch or two but not bad ones. The other boys came close.

"Will your mother let you keep it?" asked Tony.

Eric tucked the bedraggled animal inside his jacket. "Um-m," Eric was thinking of his grandmother. She disliked cats — to say the least! "Come on, anyway. Let's go home," he said.

Freddie shook his head. "I got to go to the dentist." He flashed his white teeth.

"Poor you," groaned Eric. "The dentist on a holiday! Well," he glanced at Tony, "be brave—you sure were, the way you helped me."

Freddie waved goodbye and Tony and Eric turned toward the apartment house.

It had begun to rain hard and both boys were soaking wet when they reached home. Eric felt the warmth of the kitty's body next to him. She had stopped trembling and was quiet. She likes me, he thought. I wonder if she belongs to anyone? If she only belonged to me!

Mrs. Lee heard the hall door open and feet scuffling in the hall. "My goodness, what a sight you are!" She started to help them take off their wet things.

Eric looked up, his eyes big in his damp face and his arms curved around a bulge in the front of his jacket. He seemed to be hugging himself. Tony was shifting from foot to foot and watching with questions in his eyes.

The front of Eric's jacket wiggled.

"What have you got there, Eric? A cat?" Mrs. Lee's voice was not too encouraging. He had brought cats home before, and they were usually very mangy and wild.

Eric nodded defiantly. "There was a dog after her, Mums, and she was scared. But she wasn't afraid of me. She likes me, Mums."

Mrs. Lee sighed. None of these wild cats took peaceably to apartment living and Nana disliked them so. "Well, open your coat. Don't smother the little thing."

"Can I give her some milk?" Eric asked, opening his jacket. The cat meowed plaintively and jumped to the floor, trembling and fearful.

"There, kitty, we'll not hurt you," said Mrs. Lee, and added. "Why, Eric, this one is really quite pretty! She has lovely markings, and such a nice white throat. Her eyes are beautiful—like agates. I don't believe she is a stray. She must belong to someone."

Oh, I hope not. I hope not, thought Eric as he went to fill a saucer with milk. She *feels* like my cat. She drank the milk greedily as soon as he set it in front of her and did not mind as he stroked her damp fur.

Debbie and Guido came running down the hall. "Where's the popcorn?" asked Guido.

Tony and Eric had forgotten all about it. When the others saw the cat they forgot about it, too. Nana was trying to take a nap but she came from her room to see what caused the commotion. "Another cat, Letty? Haven't you learned your lesson yet?"

"Can he keep her, Mrs. Lee?" asked Tony, watching the milk disappear. Eric waited hopefully, but Nana set her mouth in silent disapproval. Mother glanced from one to the other.

"We'll have to see," she answered. Then looking out of the window where the rain was pouring in an angry deluge, she added, "At least, she can stay until the rain stops. Where's the box we try to keep them in when they are not climbing curtains?"

"It's in my closet," Eric cried, rushing down the hall. "It's still got the old pillow in it, too. I'll put her in that."

Strangely enough the new-found cat sank into the box and, curling herself into a round ball, fell instantly to sleep.

"She was very tired," said mother. "Now all of you play quietly so as not to disturb her. I'll give you some cookies since Eric didn't get the popcorn." Such peace reigned in Eric's room after that, Mrs. Lee looked at Nana and smiled. But Nana shook her head.

"You needn't think *that* will last!" she said.

The kitty was still sleeping when Mr. Lee came home. Eric dragged him by the coat sleeve. "Come and see my new cat," he begged before his father had hardly hung up his coat. Dad kissed mother and raised his eyebrows at Nana who was setting the table.

"Well, it's his for the night," Mother admitted. Then they all looked into the box and the little cat seemed to realize that she was being inspected and opened her tawny eyes. She *was* beautiful. Her markings were of a tigerish sort and she had a large, fluffy tail.

"I'm going to call her Agate," said Eric.

"Now, just a minute." Mother was afraid this was going too far. "She's probably got a name. This is a nice kitty, not a stray. She must belong to someone. Some other child may be feeling badly over the loss of her. You'll have to take her back where you found her tomorrow, Eric, and see if she won't find her way home."

Eric felt his heart sink. She's not anybody else's cat. She's mine!, he longed to say. He said a secret prayer before he went to bed: Please,

Lord, let Agate not be anybody else's. Let her be my cat! He woke once during the night and felt something warm against his leg. The kitty had climbed out of the box and was sleeping with him!

But in the morning on his way to school he put her down by the bush where he had found her. She was so soft and warm, he just hated to let her go. She looked up at him and even followed a few steps as he started to school. She seemed forlorn and deserted when he left her.

"What did you do with the kitty? Did your mother let you keep her?" asked Freddie while he and Eric were hanging up their coats in class.

"No, Mother was afraid she belonged to someone else. She made me put her back under the same bush this morning so she can find her way home."

"But she doesn't belong to anybody," Freddie said. "I know that cat. She was Sally Duncan's and they moved away. They gave the kitty to the grocery but Mr. Critten doesn't want her either. He's got enough cats already."

Eric's heart flew up on wings. He wanted to squeeze Freddie. He wanted to rush right out and get Agate that minute but Miss French's voice called, "Into your seats, girls and boys."

Eric could hardly wait through the long morning for noon to come. Everything he did was wrong. He was the first one out of the building when the bell rang. He paid no attention to his line or anything else, but went straight to look for *his* cat.

He looked under the bush—all the bushes. He looked through the whole yard and all around the school. "Here, kitty. Here, kitty!" he called, but there was no sign of her. He ran down to the grocery and asked Mr. Critten if she had come there. Mr. Critten shook his head.

"Haven't seen her in a couple of days. She's timid, kinda scared of the noise in the store here. If you can give her a good home, I'll be glad."

The other children were returning to school when Eric finally went home. I'll look for her this afternoon. I'll look for her everywhere until I find her, he said to himself.

Mrs. Lee was watching for him anxiously when he came into the apartment. "Where have you been? There's hardly time for you to eat your lunch, Eric!" she cried.

The whole story burst out of him in a flood

91

of words as he took off his cap and coat. A small smile grew about his mother's lips. She took him by the hand and led him down to his room.

There was Agate peacefully asleep in the box!

"Mums! Mums! Where did you find her?" cried Eric as he sank down on his knees and put his face to the sleeping cat.

"You'll never guess," laughed Mother. "She was inside of the washing machine when I went into the basement to do my laundry this morning. She must have climbed in the cellar window looking for you."

"Can I keep her, Mums? Can I?"

Mother smiled. "As long as she is contented here," she agreed.

No one could have been more contented than Agate. She ate daintily and she slept companionably on Eric's bed, and was very neat about her habits. She grew more beautiful all the time. Dad, to Eric's delight, made many sketches of her.

"Why don't you put those on a calendar, Dad?" he asked. "They are swell!" His father looked at the drawings thoughtfully, and smiled.

Mother even found Agate in Nana's lap being petted one day. "She seems to take to me,"

Nana said, "though I've never liked cats."

However, Eric liked her wonderfully well. Prayers do get answered, he thought, they really do! Let Tony get all the dogs he wants. Agate is the pet for me!

He went to his calendar and put a "W—" on February 23. Always and forever F-23 would mean "wonderful" to him.

The Spelling Contest

ERIC AWOKE WITH THE sound of the wind tearing at his windows. My, it feels good to be tucked inside under the covers and hear that old wind blow, he thought. He snuggled deeper into his bed, feeling Agate warm against his feet.

He was half asleep again when he heard his mother's voice. "Eric, Eric! Time to get up." She came in and opened the Venetian blinds so that streaks of sunlight fell across the room.

94

"It's a real March day. My, how the old leaves blow—and there goes someone's hat!"

Eric was up with a bound. "Where? Whose is it?"

Mother leaned forward. "There it goes. It's Mr. Steel's. Look, he's got it—no, there it goes again! Oh, Mr. Felipe has it." She laughed. "What a wind. Now, hurry and get dressed." She kissed the top of his head and went to the kitchen.

Eric stretched and yawned and sat down on his bed again. He patted Agate curled up at the foot. She looked so cunning with one paw over her eyes. My, how she could sleep. She slept all of the time, it seemed. It must be nice to be a cat and curl in a ball and sleep as much as you liked. He tried curling in a ball. Um-m, it's a pretty good way to sleep—if I only had a tail to wind around my head.

"Eric!" his mother looked into his room. "Get up right away. Breakfast is almost ready. You'll be late to school!"

School. Eric opened sleepy eyes. That reminded him. Today they were going to have a spelling contest in class. The girls against the boys. The Secret Three had marked the day

"M-16 Win" because they had made up their minds they were going to know all the words and beat the girls all hollow!

Eric got up and opened the speller he had brought home yesterday. The word he had a hard time remembering was "listen." He was never sure whether it should be "lissen" or "listen." And "which." It sounded like "wich" to him even though Miss French said "wh-h-ich" in a way that should remind him.

"Accept"—I accept your invitation. "Except" —all except you. He could usually tell those by the way Miss French pronounced them.

Oh, boy, if we can only beat those girls, Eric was thinking. Robbie is a good speller. He'll get a bunch of them down. And I know the words pretty well, too. Lis-*t*-en.

"Eric Lee!" his grandmother was at the door. "You haven't put on a stitch of clothing yet! If I were your mother, I'd have a record made and play it every morning: " 'Oh, Eric, won't you pleased get dressed! Oh, Eric, won't you please get dressed! Oh, Eric—' "

Eric held his hands over his ears. "All right. All right. You aren't dressed either. I bet I'll beat you!"

"It's a bet." Nana dashed back to her room and Eric began jumping into his underwear. He grinned. Nana was fun. They reached the breakfast table at the same moment but Eric slid into his seat faster.

"Ha, I won!" He began devouring his cereal and telling them all about the spelling contest at the same time. Tony rang the doorbell before breakfast was finished.

"Did you study your words, Tony?" Eric asked.

"Sure, sure. But guess what? Papa found a house on Long Island and he's taking Mama and the other kids over to see it today. Shucks, I wish Guido and I didn't have to go to school."

Eric felt something heavy in his stomach. He, looked at Tony and said, "Are you going to move, then—right away?"

"Depends—" said Tony, "depends on whether Mama likes it and how much it costs."

Gee, I hope she doesn't like it, Eric thought. But he didn't say anything. He knew how anxious the Felipes were for more room. And he knew how happy he would feel if his family could find a house in Fairport.

The news rather took the edge off the spelling contest, however, and it wasn't until Miss

French was actually lining the boys and girls up on opposite sides of the class that Eric began to get excited again.

He wouldn't have admitted it—not over his dead body—but he rather liked his classroom and tall Miss French with her dark red hair. The desks in rows, the flowers on the window sill, the experiment table where they were raising caterpillars, the map of America he and Tony had drawn on the blackboard in colored chalk. Everything was part of him in a way. He was as glad as anyone to get out of work but there was something *interesting* about school.

Miss French turned toward the boys.

"M-16 Win," Eric whispered to Tony. Miss French frowned at him.

"First word," she said. "Thomas—'move.' I am going to move away." That struck Eric's funny bone. He grinned and whispered to Tony, "I wish he would move instead of you!"

"Eric!" Miss French's voice was sharp. "Anyone who wishes to whisper can take his seat right now!"

Eric turned red and straightened up. He didn't want to be put down without spelling at all and give the girls a greater chance. He paid attention and when his word came it was an easy one: "Letter." He breathed more easily. One girl and two boys were down already. Debbie spelled "whether" right, then Tony got "which."

It's w-h-i-c-h, Eric was thinking.

Tony spelled "w-h-i-c-h." Phew! He must have heard him thinking. Eric grinned. M-16 Win!

Down the row went the words back and forth to the girls and boys. By the time it was Eric's turn again there were five boys down and four girls.

"Listen!" said Miss French. "I listen to the music."

"L - i - s" began Eric. Is it 't' or is it 's?' went flashing through his mind. "t -en."

"Right," smiled Miss French.

"Whee!" Eric let out his breath in relief. "I was afraid of that one," he said to Tony before he thought.

"Eric, take your seat for whispering. I warned you." Miss French's voice was severe.

Darn, darn, darn! Eric was so mad he felt like swallowing his tongue. It was so hard for him to keep still when he ought to. That part of school was hard, hard! Now the girls were winning. Tony missed "carriage" and Freddie missed "stature" but good old Robbie was still there. He spelled down all the girls except Debbie.

" 'Accept.' I accept your invitation to the party. Debbie."

"A-x-c-e-p-t," she said. Eric felt a little sorry for her but the boys could hardly keep from cheering. They looked at Robbie excitedly.

Robbie's forehead was damp. He wet his lips.

"E-x-c-e-p-t," he spelt nervously.

Miss French closed her book. "Both wrong. It's a tie between the girls and boys. Eric, how do you spell 'accept'?"

"Ac-c-e-p-t," he answered.

"Right. But Eric, we have to learn other things besides spelling in school. We have to learn to be fair. It is not fair for one person to whisper when no one else is allowed to do so. If everybody whispered, what kind of a spelling match would we have?"

Eric went glumly home. He hadn't meant not to be fair. It was just hard not to talk. When a thought popped into his head it usually popped right out of his mouth at the same time.

"Mums! Mums!" he called as he entered.

His grandmother poked her head out of the kitchen. "Your mother went downtown. How was the spelling match?"

Eric scowled. "I got sent to my seat for whispering. It was a tie."

Nana shook her head. "You'll have to try harder next time."

"What do I smell, Nana?" Eric went into the kitchen and saw a beautiful chocolate cake with thick, gooey icing. "Oh, boy!" His fingers dipped into some frosting which had run off the plate.

Nana picked up a rolling pin and menaced him. "Wash your hands and eat your lunch first! And I've news for you," his grandmother called. "Agate is going to have kittens!"

Eric grinned and went singing down the hall. "Oh, I'm going to Alabama with my banjo on my knee!"

Agate and Her Kittens

KITTENS! KITTENS! KITTENS! Eric went around thinking, singing and talking kittens until everyone was tired of hearing about them and they had not even arrived yet.

"What on earth are you going to do with kittens in an apartment, Letty?" Nana asked. "You *would* take in a stray cat! How will you ever manage?

Mrs. Lee laughed. "Let's wait and see," she said.

It was April and Eric felt so lazy that he hated to go back to school after lunch. What if the kittens came while he was gone? He yawned widely and his mother smiled.

"I feel the same way. I guess we've got spring fever. It is a good thing the Easter holidays come soon. And that reminds me—will you come with me Saturday to fix the flowers at church? There will be a number of ladies there but we'll need some boys to help put the potted plants in the right places."

Eric nodded. He liked to help with things around the church and at Easter it was lovely there.

"The magnolia blossoms on the big trees have never been so beautiful, and just look at that forsythia! I love this time of year, don't you?" Mrs. Lee left the lunch table, and Eric followed. Spring always made him think of Fairport. He sighed. He had tried to make his mother promise that they would go this summer, but she had said they had to wait and see. Heck! He was tired of waiting. He wanted to be sure.

Eric put on his jacket to go back to school. It was too warm to wear a hat. He scowled at the sky. "Do you think it is going to rain, Mums?"

"It's hard to tell," replied his mother. "There was a verse in my reader at school which I have never forgotten. It went;

When April was asked if she could
    Make reliable weather,
She laughed 'til she cried
    And said, "Bless you, I've tried,
But things do get so mixed up together."

Agate came strolling into the kitchen and rubbed herself against Eric's leg—a sure sign that she would like something to eat. Eric smoothed her arched back.

"Do you think the box I fixed will be all right for the kittens, Mums?" He stroked the cat's soft, sleek fur. She slanted her big yellow-green eyes at him and said,

"Meow," very gently.

Mrs. Lee put some cat food on her plate and Agate ran quickly to eat it. Her small pink tongue lapped it up daintily.

Mrs. Lee glanced at Eric. "The box is just fine, and I think Lady Agate likes it too.

Agate walked leisurely from the kitchen and looked at Nana.

"Don't you have them in my room, young lady. I'm warning you!"

The cat's jewel eyes glittered for a moment and then, gracefully eluding Nana's outstretched arm, she slid into her room and retreated under the bed.

"Letty!" Nana cried, "get that cat out of my room! I won't have ten kittens yowling under my bed."

The doorbell rang. It was Tony calling for Eric to go back to school.

"Run along, Eric," said his mother. "Agate isn't going to have her kittens today, I'm sure."

Reluctantly, Eric went off with Tony. He was still thinking about the kittens. Tony was interested in their arrival, too. He had been promised one if his family moved into a house. However, no home had been found as yet.

When they had come back from their inspection of the house on Long Island, Mr. Felipe was indignant. He waved his arms, exclaiming:

"Perfectly absurd! Completely, utterly absurd! A lovely house, a magnificent house, right on the edge of the Sound—and not a room in it big enough for a grand piano. Can you *im-*

agine such a thing? And the people next door didn't like children. They shooed Henny, actually *shooed* him out of their yard. I wouldn't move my family into a place like that if it was the last one on earth! We are bound to find something better than that."

So the Felipes were still merrily racing around in No. 12.

"I can have one of the kittens when they come, can't I, Eric?" asked Tony as they trudged to school.

"I guess so," Eric frowned. He didn't like the idea of parting with those little creatures, even sight unseen. "But not until they are old enough to leave their mother. Not for quite a while," he said. "I hope they come on Easter. I want to watch them grow. We always get a plant at our church on Easter so we can take it home and watch it grow. Do you get a plant at your church, Tony?"

Tony nodded. "But Robbie doesn't get one. He has Passover now instead of Easter. But he has Matzos. Did he give you some? They were good."

"They sure were," Eric agreed. "His mother gave me a lot."

Easter Sunday arrived and Eric stood between his father and mother singing hymns. He liked especially "Christ the Lord is Risen today, A-a-alelu-ia!" and he liked the way the church smelled, all full of lilies.

But when the Lees arrived home there were no new kittens to greet them.

It was several nights later that the family was awakened by howls and scratchings.

"What in Sam Hill is that?" cried Dad.

It was Agate who was locked in the kitchen where mother had put the big box. She was scratching wildly on the kitchen door.

"Mums! Dad! Nana!" shouted Eric, waking the whole family. "There are five kittens and Agate is giving them a bath already!" Eric had been neglecting his calendar lately, but this day he marked with red stars—five of them.

Even Nana agreed, several days later when the kittens' fur had fluffed out and their round bright eyes were open, that they were really pretty. All of them had dark stripings like their mother and several had her lovely white throat.

"This place is like the Grand Central Station," complained Nana. "There's always a troop of boys and girls going up and down the hall!"

Debbie and her little sister Bridget, unfortunately, had chicken pox and couldn't come, so Eric put the box in Henny's wagon and hauled Agate and the kittens in front of Debbie's windows so they could look out at them.

Debbie and Bridget clapped their hands. "I like that one best," Debbie cried, pointing to the smallest which had a funny little screwed-up face.

"That's Pudding Face. I like him best, too. Mother and Dad and I named them all. This one's Tiger and this one's Stripes and this one Velvet and here's Butter because he's such a butterball."

"I like Pudding Face best," Debbie repeated.

For some reason, everyone liked Pudding Face best. He seemed to be the brightest and busiest of the lot, as well as the smallest. He was able to stand on his own little legs without squashing out flat, before any of the rest, and he was the first to learn to drink milk from a saucer. Mrs. Lee showed Eric how to dip his finger in the milk and let the little fellow lick it, then gradually get him to lick from the saucer. Half the time the kittens stepped into the plate and upset it before they could get a drink. But

they were learning. Agate climbed out of the box and managed to get some rest from them now (and they rested, too, from her constant washing!). One day Dad began to sketch them in all their different funny little poses.

Pudding Face was soon standing on his back legs and trying to climb out of the box. One afternoon Eric rushed home from school, and found Agate and all of her family busily washing and feeding in the middle of his bed.

"Now how on earth did they get up there?" he cried, calling to his mother.

"I expect Agate lifted them up by the backs of their necks," said Mrs. Lee, smiling. Nana came to see, too.

"The next thing the whole five will be scampering up and down the apartment!" she exclaimed. "I guess it is a good thing that I am going home soon." Nana always said she was going home long before she did, so no one worried much about that.

But the next thing Agate did was worse than anyone expected. She began hiding her children all over the house. She would drop them behind the bed or into the back of a closet or under Nana's chair. Maybe she thought they were going to be taken away from her and she was trying to keep them safe. Everyone went searching frantically for kittens when there were only two or three to be found in the box.

One day there was no sign of Pudding Face. His soft furry body and shiny, button eyes were nowhere to be found. Tony, Robbie and Eric looked everywhere. Mrs. Lee and Nana joined the search, too. Usually, they could hear a plaintive little "Meow" from a hidden kitten if they waited and listened long enough. But there was no sound from Pudding Face.

"Oh, where can he be?" cried Eric. "Where did you put him, Agate?" Agate's jeweled eyes gave no answer. Eric felt he was too old to cry but if something had happened to Pudding Face . . . It was Dad who found him when he came home for dinner, in the back of his dresser drawer. The small body was still warm but there seemed to be no life in it. Agate must have dropped the little fellow into it when no one was looking. Then the drawer had been closed and no sound from the kitten could be heard outside.

Eric was so angry he wanted to strike Agate, then he wanted to find out who shut the drawer so he could be angry about that. He wanted to hit somewhere and didn't know where to hit. It was a good thing that Dad was home because no one else could have helped Eric. Dad put his arm about him.

"Sometimes even men cry," he said gently, "when things they don't understand happen to someone they love. But they don't blame others. Agate was only trying to hide her kitten to keep it safe and no one wanted it to come to harm. It just happened." So Eric put his head on his father's shoulder and cried hard.

Suddenly he heard a little gasp. All this while Mr. Lee had been gently pressing up and down upon Pudding Face's tiny lungs. The gasp was from the kitten. Eric raised his face and watched through wet eyes. The spark of life had been caught in time. Pudding Face was breathing again!

"Oh, Dad! Oh, Mums! Oh!" was all that Eric could say.

"And now," Mrs. Lee said later, when everybody was back to normal again, "I think we had better give all but one of the kittens to your friends before we have more trouble. Either they are bothering Agate, or she thinks they are big enough to take care of themselves. After all, they can drink from a saucer now. One kitten will keep her from missing them. You can go around and visit them the way Nana does her grandchildren. That will be fun, too."

Eric started to protest but thought better of it. They had all had a real scare. After this they would keep a sharp lookout for Pudding Face, for of course they would keep him. "Debbie can have Velvet, and Robbie, Stripes, and Dick can have Butter. Tony can have Tiger, if his mother will let him. With so many children a kitten wouldn't be very safe unless they find a house."

The Secret Three Ball Team

MAY WAS A busy and exciting month. Nana finally decided that she just must go visit Uncle Dave in Kentucky for a while and see how his family was getting on. So with a great hustle and bustle, and after hunting for glasses lost, pocketbook misplaced and running back for the forgotten umbrella, Eric and his father and mother finally got her on the train.

As she kissed Eric goodbye, she asked;

"Will you miss me when I am away?"

"I sure will," Eric said, hugging her hard.

"Oh, go 'long. I know what you'll miss—my chocolate cakes!"

"Yes, I will," grinned Eric. But that wasn't all. When Nana was gone there really did seem to be an emptiness about the apartment. Mother and Dad and Eric were always starting to tell her something—and she wasn't there.

It was in the early part of May, too, that the Felipes finally found a house. To Eric's delight it was right in Hilldale, not more than a mile from the apartment house. He was happy to know that as long as the Felipes were going to move it would not be *too* far away. He went up with them to Pretty Street to the new home. It was a large, rambling place with six bedrooms, an enormous living room (space for *two* grand pianos if they wanted them), a wide, curving stairway with a wonderful bannister for sliding down, an attic and a basement and, it seemed, loads of other rooms besides. The people who were selling the house also wished to sell some of the furnishings. "Which is grand for us," said Mrs. Felipe. "Especially the big old beds!"

Guido was to have his own room—with a lock and key, if he liked. He went around with a smile all day, just planning what he was going to do when he got his *own* room! But the Felipes were not moving until June. Before then, Maria was to have her First Communion and Tony was going to play at a recital. He had to do a lot of practicing on the piano to get ready for it.

*   *   *

Maria looked so sweet and pretty all dressed up in white for her First Communion. Eric and Robbie watched her going off proudly to St. Joseph's, walking between Tony and Guido. Maria turned and waved her bouquet at them and they waved back.

"Do you have a First Communion in your church, Robbie?" Eric asked. "I get confirmed when I am twelve and then I'll take communion, mother says."

Robbie shook his head. "No, but I have a Bar Mitzvah when I am thirteen. It's kind of like it, I guess."

Eric nodded and they both felt very serious for a minute.

117

Eric was surprised to see his father walking up the sidewalk. He ran to meet him. "Hi, Dad!" he called. "What are you doing home so early?"

Mr. Lee smiled. "I just finished something and I had to come home to show you and mother —if you think you could spare me five minutes of your valuable time."

"Sure," grinned Eric, "come on, Robbie," and the pair of them followed his father into the apartment. Then, Eric's mother came in and, with an air of great importance, Mr. Lee spread out six paintings of cats and kittens. There was a portrait of Agate rolled into a ball with one paw over her eyes, and there she was stretched out on the bed with her family. There in different poses were Butter, Tiger, Stripes, Velvet and little Pudding Face.

They all looked real enough to purr.

"Oh, Dad, these are good! Are they for your calendar? I wish I had one right now," cried Eric.

Robbie was excited, too. "Say, Mr. Lee, can I have one when they're printed?"

And Mrs. Lee leaned over Dad's shoulder. "You've really got something! Have you shown them to anyone?"

Dad nodded. "Mr. White is definitely interested." Eric's eyes opened wide. "Dad, would
you—would you make a lot of money if Mr.
White bought these for a calendar?" Dad smiled
and looked from him to Robbie, who also seemed
bursting to know.

"Yes, sir. I ought to get a thousand dollars
for the set of them!"

"Yippee!" shouted Eric, and Robbie made a
gasping sound. "Then can we go to——"

"Are you trying to say Fairport by any
chance?" asked Dad.

Eric's eyes answered him.

"Yes, by Jiminy, we go to Fairport," Dad
cried. Mother looked at the pile of bills by the
telephone but Dad picked her up and swung
her around. "There'll be enough for those,
too!" He took hold of Eric and Robbie, and in
a minute they were all going around in a circle
laughing and dancing.

Agate and Pudding Face raced in and ran
madly around the room until everyone had to
stop.

Fairport! Fairport! Eric sang to himself as
he went to sleep that night. I can hardly wait!

It was in May, too, that the Secret Three Ball

Team had been formed. The boys had so much extra energy it seemed they had to do *something* to work it off. At first, after school, Eric and Robbie (Tony was usually practicing) went over to the lot where Tommy Haines, Billy Henski and the rest of the big boys were playing ball. Robbie was a great baseball fan and he could play pretty well. He and Eric stood around on the edge of the field watching for a while. When the ball went beyond the players, into the bushes, they went scrambling after it.

"All right! All right!" cried Tommy at last. "You guys can field if you want."

Eric and Robbie grinned and worked like beavers, chasing balls. Tommy and Billy even let them get their licks at bat once in a coon's age. It wasn't so easy to hit the ball with all the big boys watching, even if you put your tongue between your teeth and swung with all your might.

Eric and Robbie went home for dinner tired and a little discouraged.

"We ought to have a ball team of our own," Eric said to Robbie one day, "but Tommy and Billy's gang always have the field, so where could we play?"

They walked along in silence and then Robbie's eyes brightened.

"Say," he said, wiping his hot forehead, "you know that vacant lot back of Mrs. Ryder's house? The one that has a hedge all around it. If she would let us play there, that would be a swell place! We could go into it through the woods and the big kids wouldn't know we were there."

"If they did, they'd want it themselves," Eric nodded. "But that field's got an awful lot of big weeds in it." They had played cowboys there recently so he knew.

"O.K., so what?" Robbie asked. "We could get Tony and Dick and Freddie and borrow some sickles and the lawnmower from Dad and fix it up in no time!"

Eric grew excited. He could see a beautiful diamond already, with himself hitting a home run right into the hedge! "We could call it the Secret Three Ball Ground. Do you think Mrs. Ryder would let us use it really?"

"What do you say we go ask her right after school tomorrow?" Robbie suggested.

It was quite a delegation which called on Mrs. Ryder the next day. Eric, Robbie, Tony, Dick Higgins and Debbie (how Debbie got in on it no one knew).

They were all very respectful.

"Please, Mrs. Ryder, may we use the field that's vacant with the hedge around it?"

"The big boys are always using the lot and we can't get our licks when it's our turn, so we want a team of our own!"

Mrs. Ryder looked a bit bewildered.

"You want to use the vacant lot over there?" she nodded her head in its direction. "But what for, I don't quite understand—" then seeing a bat in Robbie's hand, and a ball in Eric's she caught on. "Oh, you want to play ball there. But what about my windows?"

"We'd be very careful," said everyone at once.

"Besides," Robbie added thoughtfully, "your windows are a long way from home plate!"

"Um-m," Mrs. Ryder looked from one eager face to the other. "All right, but—your team is responsible if there's any damage done!"

"Whoopee!" they all shouted, and, "Thanks! Mrs. Ryder." And off they ran like excited rabbits to get busy clearing the field. They soon found that the lawnmower wasn't much help (after the blades had been rather badly bent by stones) and it was much harder to cut with the sickle than they thought. But by running around from base to base it wasn't long until they had that part tramped down, and whenever they lost a ball in the weeds around the edge everybody stopped playing and used the sickle until it was found again. The results were rather ragged but the main thing was that they could really play baseball without anybody yelling about "sore arms" or "your mother wants you."

Eric wrote down the line-up on paper. At first there were loud complaints about letting any girls on the team, but after Debbie and Anna Mae, a red-haired, pigtailed friend of hers, worked so hard helping to get the weeds down, they had to let them in. Then Mrs. Ryder sent over her grandson, seven-year-old Peter, and they had to let him play because, after all, it was his field. They tried to keep him chasing balls in the outfield but he wanted his turn like the rest.

"If I chase balls, I ought to get my licks at bat," he insisted. Eric and Robbie looked at one another. That's what *they* thought when *they* played with bigger boys. So they said "O.K. Peter," and to their surprise, Peter was a good lefty. He could hit. Maybe only a pop fly sometimes, but often a good solid hit.

"Say," Tony said one afternoon after they had been practicing hard, "we are getting pretty good!"

Debbie had proved to be a fast pitcher. She had a wind-up that was amazing to see. Anna Mae could run like the wind *if* she got a hit. Eric and Robbie and Tony were all learning a lot at bat, and Freddie was a good catcher. Guido was dependable wherever he was and Dick—well, as Dick said, "I guess I'm better at science," but he liked to play.

One of the boys in the Hilldale Apartments who went to a private school heard about the Secret Three team and challenged them to play the Stonefield Braves.

"But they are too good for us. They have a coach and real practice," Eric scoffed. "They'd murder us!"

"So what?" asked Robbie. "We'll get experience that way." After much argument a game was scheduled on a Saturday morning. Eric was really worried. "Gee, I hope they don't slaughter us," he groaned.

Debbie smiled at him serenely. "They won't. I've been practicing a Secret Three curve," she told him.

Mr. Klein went along to see the game and Mr. Lee wished he had. He waved from the window when he saw the S-3's returning, dirty and bedraggled but with grins on their faces.

"You look as though you had won!" he cried.

"We won a Moral Victory," Eric called exultantly.

"What's that?" His father looked puzzled.

"That's what Mr. Klein said because they didn't beat us so much—only 16 to 22! You should have seen Debbie's pitching. She scared them to death with her wind-up!"

Eric paused and looked a little embarrassed. "But I told them they ought to see my father pitch. I said you could lick 'em easy. So-o, they challenged us to bring our fathers next time. Will you go, Dad? Will you?"

Eric watched his father anxiously. Mr. Lee had often told stories of how he had carried the ball for "Rendville High" with the crowds yelling, "We want a touchdown! We want a touchdown!" or how he'd pitched a no-hit no-run game for that same school. But there was always a grin and a twinkle along with the story, so Eric felt sure it was being made up for fun. Of course, his Dad had played ball with him a lot when he was just learning to throw and catch. But this was different. This was serious. He hoped his Dad really could pitch.

His father was startled, then he grinned confidently. "Why, sure, I'll do it. Didn't I say I used to be pretty good on the mound at Rendville High. Old Steamball Lee—that's what they called me!"

Mr. Felipe, Mr. Klein, Mr. Higgins and Peter's father all agreed to play. Freddie, unfortunately, didn't have a Dad since he was an orphan and neither Debbie nor Anna Mae was allowed to be in the game because they were not sons.

"Let's be the cheering section," suggested Debbie. "You know all those kids from Stonefield school came to cheer their team. You bring your harmonica, Freddie, and Anna Mae, get your brother's drum. We'll be a band."

One of the S-3's heard some news that cheered them. The Stonefield Braves' best hitter had to go to the hospital to have his tonsils out. Eric sympathized with him, but he was glad he wasn't going to be in the game against the S-3's.

It did not seem as though the fathers had much chance to practice before the big game.

Eric and Tony and Robbie were very quiet with one another. They didn't dare to say how anxious they were about the way their fathers played.

The fatal Saturday finally arrived. It was so warm it felt more like July than May. Tiny green leaves had appeared on the winter-black branches of the trees. The robins were fat and raising families now. There were three eggs in a nest in Robbie's lilac bush. All of Hilldale seemed jubilant and gay. The S-3's and their fathers set off in high spirits for the Stonefield's ballground. Eric's Dad was so sure they were going to "plaster those fellows" that Eric began to shout and run with assurance, too. There was a funny little light in his mother's eye and she winked at him, but she was laughing with the other mothers, and didn't seem at all worried.

Debbie, Anna Mae, and Freddie with some of the other boys and girls, were on the field when they arrived. They commenced to yell and bang on drums and blow horns. Freddie was too excited to play his harmonica so he just yelled with the rest. The Stonefield Braves had a large group of rooters, too. And they yelled for their team. Mr. Felipe and Mr. Lee waved their arms at everybody, and presently the umpire blew a whistle and the game was on.

The S-3's were up at bat first. Um-m, thought Eric, that's a tough looking pitcher they have! Robbie was first at the plate. His eyes glittered and his round face was damp. He glanced at Eric and it was easy to see that he was pretty nervous. I'm glad I'm not up first! thought Eric. After two balls came three strikes and Robbie was out. He came over to the bench and shrugged.

Mr. Ryder, who followed him, flied out.

"Gotta get used to it," he said, grinning.

Mr. Felipe was up next and the very first thing gave the ball a swat and went tearing off for first base.

"Foul ball," shouted the umpire. Mr. Felipe pulled his hair and went back to the plate. Tony was fidgeting on the bench.

Mr. Felipe swung wildly again and the ball was off to third base. Mr. Felipe ran madly and then slid full length just under the catch. He made it! The S-3's had a man on first! Everybody was yelling. The Stonefield Braves' cheerers were calling "Kill em! Murder the bums!" But Mr. Felipe shook hands with himself and waved to the cheering section on his side.

Eric was up next. His heart was beating so hard inside him that he was afraid the bat would shake. "Take it easy, son," called his Dad and his Mother waved her handkerchief. One strike, two balls, two strikes and then whang! he connected. He was down to first base like a shot but the third baseman caught Mr. Felipe at second. Three out!

"Gr-r!" groaned Mr. Felipe as he went out to the field.

Dick was up next but that was all.

The teams changed places and Eric could see that his Dad was looking a bit anxious. Debbie shouted, "Go to it, Steamball!" and he grinned at her.

He put the first batter out all right. Two balls, three strikes. And Eric breathed easier. But the second man up was a father with a professional stance, and he was on third base so fast it made them all dizzy! Now the Stonefield Braves were yelling like crazy. Three strikes and out! Hurray! Hurray! The next man got a single and the man on third came in. The Stonefield Braves had a run. Darn, darn, darn! But that was all they got that inning. One to nothing.

Well, the game had only started. And Eric, Robbie and Tony smiled at each other. Their fathers were pretty good. And what was more important, they were playing hard! It was a real game.

At the start of the sixth inning, the fathers were getting pretty tired. The score was twelve to ten in favor of the S-3's. But Eric heard Mr. Klein lean over to his Dad and say, "Boy, we sure let ourselves in for something, didn't we?" Mr. Klein and Mr. Lee had both made home runs in the fifth inning and they were still panting. They were glad it was only a seven-inning game.

And Mr. Felipe was wet to the skin. When he ran for a base, he really ran. But one thing was sure. The fathers on the Stonefield Braves team were just as hot and perspiring.

Eric patted his Dad's back. "We've got them on the run, now, Dad," he crowed. He didn't feel a bit tired. He had got a three base hit in the fifth, and Tony had whacked a single to bring him home. He was feeling pretty good, even if he was hot.

Debbie and her group were so hoarse that Freddie could play his harmonica and actually be heard. The mothers were mopping their foreheads with their handkerchiefs and wondering why they hadn't thought to bring some cases of pop.

Unfortunately, the Braves got four runs off Mr. Lee in the last of the sixth. Eric and Tony groaned. 14-12 in favor of the Braves! And Dick was first up in the first of the seventh. Then Peter, Mr. Higgins and Robbie.

To everyone's complete astonishment, Dick sent the ball flying into the field and made it to first. Peter struck out but Mr. Higgins, Dick's father, got a two base hit. Dick was on third and his father on second. It was up to Robbie. Robbie gritted his teeth and took hold of the bat. Strike one!

Robbie shook his head.

Ball one.

Strike two—oh, Robbie! Everybody was holding his breath.

The ball was pitched, and socko! Robbie gave it everything! In came Dick, in came Mr. Higgins, in came Robbie. Three runs and only one man out! Peter's father was up next and he was

walked. There was a consultation and it was
decided to put in a pinch hitter for Mr. Felipe.
Freddie. Freddie grinned all over his face.

Strike one. Where did that ball go?

Strike two. Freddie took a new hold on the
bat.

Ball one.

Ball two. Come on Freddie. Last chance.

The ball was pitched and Freddie hit it.

Down he went like a streak of lightning and
was safe on first. Peter's father was on second.
Two men on, and one out. Eric was up. His
heart was racing.

Ball one.

He fouled the next one.

Strike one. A fast throw to second caught Mr.
Ryder off the bag. Two outs.

Eric could see the pitch coming at him. A

beauty. Wham! Off it went. Freddie was home —but Eric was out at third base.

O.K. Now the score was 16-14 in favor of the S-3's. It was up to Dad.

The first Brave came to bat. Strike one! Ball one. Ball two. Strike two. Strike three. OUT! How everyone was yelling. Boys were hugging each other in excitement.

"Come on, Steamball," Eric heard his mother shout.

Dad was really putting the steam on. Unfortunately, the next Brave bunted safely, and made first base.

The next hit, a pop fly, and Mr. Felipe caught the ball and made a double play! The S-3's had won. Hurray! Hurray!

What a day! Eric marked it with red ink on his calendar. May 27th. That was one to remember.

He felt very proud of "Old Steamball." In fact, the Secret Three were very well satisfied with all their Dads.

The Felipes Moving Day

June came, and all Hilldale was lush and green. The hedges were full of chirping birds and Eric made Agate wear a collar with a bell on it to give them warning of her tiger-like approach. The boys and girls had begun to sing, "Three more weeks and we'll be free from this school of misery—" as generations of boys and girls had done before them.

And finally the day arrived for the Felipes to move. From early morning there was so much going on across the hall that Eric kept racing back and forth, trying not to be in the way but not wanting to miss anything. He could not help a little unhappy feeling inside himself. It

135

would not be the same with the Felipes gone from their apartment. Another thought kept nagging at him. In spite of his father's high hopes for the kitten calendar, it had not yet been sold and no plans for going to Fairport were being mentioned. Eric had started to say something several times, but the look in his mother's eyes had warned him to be silent. Reluctantly, he had come to believe there would be no going away for him this summer.

So, unhappily, he watched the Felipes moving.

Mr. Felipe had bought most of the beds in the big house, and the first thing the family did was to pile all the bed linen into the station wagon and take it up to the house on Pretty Street. Then Mrs. Felipe and Bessie made up the beds there.

"Oh, I feel as though we live here already!" cried Mrs. Felipe. Her dishes and kitchen pans had been arranged the day before. She rushed back to the apartment for more things.

But where were the moving men? "The moving men haven't come yet!" Tony fairly shouted at Eric. He was so excited, his hair was tangled up all over his head. It was eleven o'clock.

Mr. Felipe went to the phone to call the movers.

136

"This is completely unorthodox," he cried. "Your men should have been here at eight o'clock! Where is the van? What utterly impossible reason is there for not being here now? What! You say I didn't—but, I'm sure,—I—I—" Mr. Felipe's anger died to a weak little flame. "Oh," he said at last and hung up the receiver.

"Now what?" asked Mrs. Felipe. Eric and Tony were as still as statues waiting to hear what had happened.

"Well, dear," began Mr. Felipe lamely, "It seems I was to let them know *definitely* and apparently I didn't let them know *definitely* that I wanted to move today. The vans have gone somewhere else!"

Mrs. Felipe felt behind her for a clear space on the couch and sat down. "Now what are we going to do?" she cried. "All this mess and it's Saturday, which means we'll have to wait until Monday—like this!"

"Never you mind, dear. I'll get a mover. If it is the last act of my life on this green earth, I'll get a mover for us today." He grabbed his hat and rushed out of the apartment before anyone could say a word.

Twelve o'clock, one o'clock came and Mr.

Felipe had not returned with any movers. Mrs. Lee invited Tony, Guido, Maria and Henny over to have lunch with Eric. The baby, Donato, was with Bessie up on Pretty Street. Mrs. Felipe said she was much too upset to eat. But she was grateful for the pot of hot coffee Eric carried over to her. She just set it on a packing case in front of her and drank it there. At the Lee's it was like a picnic with all of the Felipes shouting around the table.

After lunch, Maria, seeing her mother so frantic, decided to do something about it.

She knew where there was a big yellow truck. She would go there and ask the man to help them to move. Carefully she put on her gloves and hat and took her pocket book.

"Where you going?" asked Henny, eyeing her suspiciously.

"Sh! I'm going to find a moving man for Mama. Be quiet or she won't let me go."

"I want to go, too!" cried Henny.

"Sh-h-h! You can't. It's a long way to walk."

"I wanna go. I wanna go!" wailed Henny.

Maria put her hand over his mouth. "All right. You can go, but if you get tired, you'll be sorry!" She wiped his face and put on his jacket. They slipped by their distracted mother and set off importantly on their errand.

At two o'clock, Mr. Felipe phoned that he thought he had found some movers and that they would be there soon. Neither the movers nor Mr. Felipe had arrived by three. Mrs. Lee asked why they didn't wait until Monday to move but Mrs. Felipe only shook her head. She felt as though they just had to go, with everything in such a muddle.

"I suppose Maria and Henny are at your house?" she asked Eric's mother. Mrs. Lee was surprised.

"No, Guido and Tony are in Eric's room, but the little ones left right after lunch," she said. "Perhaps they are outside playing. I'll send Eric to look."

"Ask Tony to round them up, please," Mrs. Felipe answered distractedly. "I'll send them up to Bessie as soon as Mr. Felipe gets here with the car."

Eric, Tony and Guido all went to look for Maria and Henny. Tony searched the playground, Eric looked in the field and Guido began systematically to ring the doorbells of all their friends. But no Maria and Henny were rounded up.

Mrs. Felipe was really anxious when the boys reported to her. She tried to think when she had seen them last. "It must have been over an hour ago!"

"I saw them then," Eric told her. "They were going down the sidewalk and they were all dressed up."

"All dressed up?"

"Yes, Maria had on her hat and gloves and Henny had on his best coat."

"Now where on earth were they going, do you suppose? Oh, I wish Vincent would come home. It's going to be too late to move now. We shall just have to take what we can in the station wagon and manage the best way possible."

Mrs. Felipe wandered up and down rubbing her hands together. She didn't dare to leave the apartment for fear she'd miss a call from her husband.

"Are you boys sure you've been to everybody they know?" asked Mrs. Lee.

Guido thought carefully. "Well, maybe I missed Mrs. Shumacher. They go there sometimes."

"Well, run there quickly and see," cried Mrs. Felipe.

"They may have gone to the library or to the stores," suggested Eric. "Maria had her pocketbook. Tony and I could go down Hilldale Avenue and look."

Mrs. Felipe could only nod.

Eric and Tony set off running down Hilldale Avenue. "This reminds me of when we were little, remember Tony? I took a dollar out of my mother's pocketbook. I didn't know any better then. Remember all the stuff we bought? We ate so much we didn't have enough to get home on the bus and the bus man let us ride free. Gee, we were crazy when we were little!"

"Let's go into the library first," Tony said. So they entered the attractive brick building in back of P.S. 81. Miss Cruse, the librarian, said, no, she had not seen Maria and Henny, but they looked into the children's room just to be sure. Maria and Henny were not there but the boys noticed a lot of new books.

"Say, this one about cowboys is neat," Eric exclaimed, but Tony was interested in a big book filled with pictures of sailing ships. After a while they suddenly looked at one another.

"Well, Maria and Henny aren't here. We'd better go to some stores," Eric said, guiltily clos-

141

ing his book on the Bar WD Ranch. The pair slipped quickly out of the library, shutting the door quietly behind them. They ran as fast as they could go to Mr. Critten's grocery.

"We bought cookies here that time," Tony said. "Have you any money, Eric?"

"I've got a quarter but I'd rather have a comic book," Eric replied. "Mr. Critton, have you seen Maria and Henny anywhere? They've been gone from home a long time."

"Those little ones run away? Didn't see 'em. You keep right after them, boys. My little fellow ran off once. Somebody found him and took him to the police station. If you don't find 'em, ask the police, why—" and Mr. Critton went into great detail about his little fellow and the police station.

Tony and Eric hurried on to Sid's drug store. A row of children were there sitting on the high stools having ice cream, but not Maria and Henny. Both Eric and Tony were rather tired by this time so they refreshed themselves with chocolate popsicles and looked over Sid's supply of new comics. Before they left they asked Sid to call their mother if the runaways showed up.

"You'd better keep right after them or else call the police," Sid advised, and his friendly brown eyes were concerned.

"Say, this is getting serious," Eric frowned. "Where shall we go now? Down to the park? That's where you and I headed the day we went."

"O.K." agreed Tony, "only we better hustle. What if something has happened to them?" All this talk about the police was beginning to bother him. Eric felt the same way. They began running again, branching off Hilldale and hurrying down Montague to the big public park.

It was a large, sprawling park "But they would only go to the little playground. That's the only place they know," Tony felt sure. They were not anywhere to be seen among the swings and slides of the little playground.

"I really think we *ought* to ask a policeman!" Eric's eyebrows were high and anxious. "Gee whiz, it's getting late."

The policeman on the corner listened to them intently. "What, kids run away again? How long have they been gone? Since near one o'clock —say, it's almost six now!" Eric and Tony were amazed that the time had gone so fast. "Just

a minute. Officer Patrick will be along here in a cruise car and I'll get him to help you."

Even as he spoke the white and green police car came in sight. A blast on the whistle brought it to a halt. There were two men in it and Officer Patrick leaned from the window.

"What's up, Sullivan?" he asked.

"A couple of runaways, sir," said Sullivan.

"What? These two running away?"

"No, smaller than these. A boy three and a girl five. This pair is the search party."

"Fine. Hop in the car, boys, and give us a description of the little ones. We'll help you find them. Have they been reported?"

"We don't know," gulped Eric and Tony. The idea of getting into the cruise car quite overwhelmed them. Sailing along they felt like detectives or something!

"Better check with headquarters," Officer Patrick told Officer Riley. Officer Riley picked up the phone. "Car No. 16 reporting. Officer Riley. We have a pair of boys looking for a lost brother and sister. Anything on the register? Name Felipe."

"Station 6 to Car No. 16. Yes, sir, get those kids home. The little ones came back long ago and the mother wants those two immediately!"

"Check!"

Eric and Tony looked at each other sheepishly. Now they were the ones being hunted instead of Maria and Henny!

Nevertheless, they felt important when the cruise car swung up in front of the apartment house. Officer Patrick had scolded them mildly for not getting in touch with Mrs. Felipe sooner but he blew the siren and deposited them with a flourish before their friends.

As luck would have it, Debbie, Robbie and Dick and a number of others were standing there watching furniture (which Tony soon discovered to be his) being loaded into an old van. Their mouths dropped open when they saw Eric and Tony get out of the squad car.

"Thank you for bringing us home, Officer Patrick and Officer Riley," cried the boys.

"Don't mention it," replied the men, "just get in there and let your mothers know you are home."

"Gee gosh!" cried Robbie. "How come you get a ride with the police? What have you been doing?"

"Oh, we were just in a hurry to get home," Eric answered airily.

Debbie smiled a little. "Yes, and you better

hurry some more," she said. "Your mothers are awful mad."

The pair turned and ran. They almost bumped into two men moving a chest of drawers on a dolly. They were complaining bitterly. "Never seen such furniture in all my born days," said one.

"What we goin' to do with that gran' pianner?" asked the other. "We ain't never moved a gran' pianner before."

Mr. Felipe pounced upon Tony. "Thank goodness you are back! Mama mia! Everything has happened this day! Your mother is in a tail spin with so much to do. Where in the name of Aloysius have you been?"

"We were just looking for Maria and Henny," Tony said meekly. "Where were they, anyhow?"

"They went to a gas station. Maria thought the big oil truck could help move us. And it probably could do as good a job as the ones I found! These men don't know the first thing about moving and now they are asking for more money. Call your mother, Tony."

Eric came to the apartment door. "Mother says to come over and have something to eat, Tony and Mr. Felipe."

Mr. Felipe pulled his thick hair straight up. "Maybe I could eat, but I could not swallow!" he cried.

* * *

The Lees talked for weeks afterwards about the Felipes' moving day. While the men were still taking the furniture out piece by piece, it had begun to rain. Then they had refused to move another stick without a lot more money. Mr. Felipe had argued and bargained until ten o'clock at night and then they had begun to move again. By that time it was really pouring. The grand piano was maneuvered into the truck under a heavy tarpaulin about three o'clock in the morning. "My poor piano will never be the same again!" wailed Mrs. Felipe.

The last load was finally carried to Pretty Street at daybreak.

"Wherever did Mr. Felipe get those movers?" asked Mr. Lee.

"Goodness knows," laughed Eric's mother, "but he had made up his mind to move and move they did. I'm glad they didn't have to move very far."

"And so were the moving men," Mr. Lee chuckled.

But Eric didn't chuckle. He had looked into the empty apartment and it didn't seem possible it could be so deserted. Nothing but a few old broken toys instead of all the Felipes who were so much fun.

That afternoon he and Robbie sat alone in the S-3 hut and wondered if Tony would come back often to play. Robbie was going away to camp for the summer and so were Dick and Freddie. Of the gang, only Eric would be left. If only his family were planning to go away, too, to Fairport and the sea.

"Didn't your father sell the paintings of the cats for the calendar, Eric?" Robbie asked. Eric shook his head and felt completely miserable.

A Birthday and a Barn

ON SUNDAY, June 11th, Eric was ten years old. Halfway to twenty. He opened his eyes and looked at the much marked-up Secret Three calendar on his bulletin board. It didn't seem such a long time since he was nine, and yet he felt as though it would be forever before he was eleven. It was funny how, when a year was past, it was a short year and when it was ahead, it was very long.

Presents! He hopped out of bed, upsetting Agate and Pudding Face asleep on the foot, and began opening the packages on his table. The two cats jumped on the table top, too, and inquisitively poked into the boxes and tissue paper.

"Gee, a swell baseball glove!" Eric socked his fist into the big leather mitt. "That's what I wanted all right." He laughed at the card which said,

"From one Steamball to another. Lots of love, Dad."

He pulled the wrappings from a second package. The card read, "Love and kisses, Mums."

Inside were a new sweater and some new materials for his construction—nice, new strips of balsa wood and two bottles of airplane glue. He wanted to begin working on some new models only somehow his heart was not in the work just now. He put the package aside and reached for another. Agate had already curled herself up in the middle of his glove and Pudding Face was tearing back and forth through some tissue paper on the floor.

The third present was from Nana. Oh, boy, books! *Lone Wolf on Timber Trail, The Boy*

Scouts in the Northwest, Brick Williams of BX Ranch. They sounded great! He turned to the first page of the second title and began to read.

"Happy Birthday to You! Happy Birthday to you!" His mother and father sang coming into his room. Kisses from Mums and spanks from Dad until he squealed "That's enough! Give me air. Thanks, Dad, for the glove. It's swell, and Mums, the sweater is neat and thanks for the balsa wood, too. Look, what Nana sent —three books!"

The family went to the early morning service at their church together and Eric listened for his name to be mentioned because the Reverend Barry always asked a blessing for you on your birthday. And sure enough, he heard, "And we ask a special blessing for Eric on this, his birthday."

As they were leaving church after the service, the minister shook his hand hard and gave his shoulder a friendly push.

"Ten years old! Getting pretty grown up, I should say. We'll be having a full-sized man in church soon. Eat a big piece of cake for me."

Eric liked to look into the eyes of the Reverend Barry. They were warm and friendly.

Eric blew out the candles on his cake at a picnic in a nearby woods that afternoon. Of course, his wish was for Fairport. All but two of the candles went out on the first blow. Did that mean he had to wait two years before his wish came true?

All the S-3 ball team were at his party. Dad had built a fire so they could cook their own wienies on long sticks which they cut from bushes.

"This makes me think of the picnic we had the day we had the snow battle," said Tony. "Remember in your room, Eric?" Eric grinned. He remembered and so did the others. There was no snow outside today. The sun sprinkled gold through the leaves to brighten the fresh green woods.

They drank gallons of pop and their faces were a combination of mustard, ketchup and chocolate frosting. Mrs. Lee handed around extra paper napkins—"Just so I can see who's behind those trimmings!" she laughed.

They played "hide and seek" and "cowboys" in the woods until they were all hot and exhausted. And there wasn't anything left to drink or eat, so it was time to say "goodbye" and go along home.

"It was a nice birthday, wasn't it?" asked Mrs. Lee when she came to hear Eric's prayers at bedtime. Eric grinned.

"It sure was." He gave her a hug. "I hope nobody got poison ivy this year! Now if only—" his eyes turned to the tiny houses he had built for his Fairport town.

His mother frowned slightly. "Well, maybe we can't have everything. You really are a pretty lucky boy, you know, just to be living in Hilldale in the good old U.S.A. with good food and clothes. When you think of the thousands of children in other parts of the world who have so much less."

"I know," Eric said, a little tired. He had heard about this before. "And I have you and Dad and all those presents"—his table was piled with the gifts his friends had brought—"and Agate and Pudding Face."

So he went into the living room and said goodnight to his father with a big hug and "Thank you for everything, Dad." Eric tried to think no more of the tide coming in to shore at Fairport. At least, he tried.

Two afternoons later Tony came home with Eric after school. The boys visited back and

155

forth as much as they could, but it was still not like having the Felipes across the hall. Eric had a lot of fun though when he went up to the house on Pretty Street. All of the children had their own bedrooms.

Guido was so happy with his. "Look, Eric," he cried, "I don't have to lock my door. I've got a closet with shelves in it and I have a lock on it that's a combination lock and doesn't need a key. Nobody knows the combination but Mother and me—but I'll tell it to you."

There was so much play space in the attic for wrestling, and in the cellar for hammering and sawing, that it was a wonderful house for the Felipes.

This time Tony was visiting Eric and going to stay for dinner. Mrs. Lee was in the kitchen and the boys in Eric's room when suddenly the front door flew open and Mr. Lee burst in like an unexpected tornado.

"I sold them! I sold them! Letty! Eric! Come here, come here!"

"What? What?" Eric came running with Agate and Pudding Face dashing under his feet.

"I sold my kitten calendar to the White Company. And I am going to get some other work

156

from them, too. Hurray, Hurray!" Dad lifted mother up high. "Stop your dinner, honey, and let's all go out to eat. Let's celebrate!"

He swung Eric up high. "It was your idea, Eric. First to do a calendar and then to do the cats!"

Eric grinned dizzily. "But you painted them, Dad," he admitted.

Tony came in with startled amazement and Mr. Lee swung him for good measure.

They were all laughing happily. Mrs. Lee straightened her hair and her apron.

"That's wonderful," she cried, "I'm so glad. But let's stay home. I've a good dinner and it's almost ready. I'll put some candles and chocolate sauce on the ice cream and make it a party!"

"Candles on ice cream? Who's crazy now?" laughed Dad but he dropped into his comfortable chair in the living room. They could go out to celebrate another night.

Eric sat on the wide arm of the chair. "I knew somebody would like those kittens, Dad. They were so real! Now you won't have to worry any more and neither will Mums." Dad looked up.

"Has she been worrying?"

Perhaps I shouldn't tell, thought Eric. "Oh, not so much," he said lightly. He sat thinking for a minute in silence. After all, Dad had said that if he sold the calendar . . . should he ask or not? He had to ask.

"Dad, do you think we can go to Fairport now?"

His father's forehead wrinkled. "You want to go pretty badly, don't you?" Eric nodded mutely.

"Um, I know I promised and you really deserve something, for it was your idea about the calendar, but it surely is late to start looking for a place to stay there. Reasonable houses are always hard to find in June. . . ." Eric's face began to fall. His Dad chucked him under the chin. "Still," he cried, "we never know until we look. I'll have Uncle Russ drive Mother and me up to Fairport this week end and we'll give the situation the once over. How's that?"

Eric threw his arms around his Dad's neck. "Oh, swell! Thanks! Thanks, thanks!"

"Now just a minute—don't let your hopes fly too high. Because we are going to look is no guarantee that we'll find anything."

"I know," Eric said, but he was tearing off to tell Tony. As far as he was concerned they were on their way to Fairport already.

He was quite unprepared for the long faces with which Mr. and Mrs. Lee returned to the apartment that Saturday evening

"We haven't given up, Eric," they told him when he flung himself upon them. "We've left our name with lots of people and they are going to see what they can do. But so far we haven't found anything we could afford—not even rooms."

His father flung his hat into his chair in disgust. "One thousand, they ask. Two thousand, they ask. As though that green stuff grew on trees!"

His mother put her arm around Eric. "We saw your friend Charley, and his mother said she'd try to find something for us. And Captain Adams said, 'Tell Eric he can bail my boats when he comes up.' Something will happen. You know, we are a good-luck family and things go right for us!"

Eric could not be comforted. He had felt so sure they would find a place. He went back to his room and lay down on the bed. Agate and Pudding Face began to play over him. Fat Pudding Face scrambled up on his stomach and Agate pushed him off. But nothing they did could make Eric laugh. He felt as though he had a big dark hole inside which nothing could fill.

For days he went around with clouds over his heart. Finally Mrs. Lee said:

"Eric, you've just got to stop looking so glum. After all, the heavens haven't fallen and it isn't as though we haven't tried our best. Now snap out of it!"

But Eric could not snap, though he tried to pretend he had. He thought of the mill pond where the crabs were waiting for his net. He thought of the channel with the raft in it where he and Charley dived. He tried not to act as though his heart was so leaden, but it was, just the same.

The last days of school dragged by. The weather was so warm that all of the teachers and the children were tired and could hardly wait for the last day to come.

Then, without any warning, a letter arrived from Fairport.

"Dear Mr. and Mrs. Lee," it started—"When you were up here two weeks ago, you asked if there were any place we knew of which you could rent for the summer. We could think of nothing at that time. However, as you know, Mr. Kerry fixed up the barn for our son Duncan to live in. Now, all of a sudden, Duncan has gotten married and moved into an apartment. So if you would like the barn, you are welcome. It is furnished for summer living, has gas and electricity and running water. Be glad to know at the earliest possible moment if you folks would care to use it. Price reasonable.

Sincerely,

Roberta Kerry."

Eric's eyebrows were up. His heart almost stopped beating.

"Would you live in a barn, Mums, would you?"

Mrs. Lee looked at him. "A barn—live in a barn? Why I think a barn for the summer would be wonderful! Didn't I say we were a lucky family?"

Although they had not been inside, the Lees knew the Kerry's big, red barn very well. It stood at the end of a lane on the edge of the Kerry lawn, surrounded by trees and backed upon an open field. It was near the shore and right on the bus line, too, so Dad could get the train to work.

"Oh, Eric, it will be perfect!" his mother cried.

Eric had not realized that his mother was as anxious as he was to go to Fairport. You could not always tell what grown-ups' real feelings were.

But when school was finally over and Eric had received his report card promoting him to the fifth grade, and the Lees were all packed up and ready to leave for Fairport (with Agate and Pudding Face meowing plaintively in their carrying cases) any one could have told how happy they all were.

Eric took a last look around his room to see if there was anything he'd forgotten to take. He saw his calendar hanging askew on the bulletin board. He put three fingers to his cheek and winked his right eye.

"That old thing surely is falling apart," he thought, "and so is the Secret Three this summer. But we'll get together again and something is going to happen on all those days the calendar has left. I wonder what?"